RISE OF THE FURY

MAC CROW THRILLER #5

CLINT HOLLINGSWORTH

Icicle Ridge Graphics

ACKNOWLEDGMENTS

To my esteemed editors,
Suzette Hollingsworth and DeLynn Elliot.
Without them, my readers would likely think I'd never
taken an English class.

OTHER BOOKS BY CLINT HOLLINGSWORTH

The Mac Crow Thrillers

#1 The Sage Wing Blows Cold, #2 Death in the High Lonesome, #3 The Deep Blue Crush,

#4 Dying to Win, #5 Rise of the Fury

Voyages of the Seeker

#1 Seeker One, #2 Seeker Two, #3 Seeker Three

The Ghost Wind Chronicles

The Road Sharks

The Wandering Ones (Graphic Novels)

#1 The Aftertime, #2 The Mad Scout, #3 The Mission, #4 The Road Home, #5 Turf War, #6 Mind Games

:

1

This was ridiculous. She was not a person to get nervous.

But she was, and she had good reason. She'd screwed up big time, colossally, and her employers were not the sort of people who tolerated incompetence, particularly when it was on a large and very public scale. If she couldn't talk her way out of this, it was like the old song said; "Odds are you won't live to see tomorrow."

She saw him as he came down the sidewalk, impeccably dressed as always. His graying mustache was waxed into sharp points, an affectation that had always amused her. Nothing amusing now. He was her mentor in the biz, and now he was looking at her like she already had a bullet in her brain as he sat down at the little table in front of her.

He pulled out a small electronic device, thumbed it on and sat it on the table between them. It would prevent anyone from listening in electronically, letting them hear only static. Before the 'incident' she doubted he would have even bothered, but now the entire organization was on high alert.

Because of her royal foul-up.

"Well, Marjory. You have certainly screwed the pooch on this one," he said. "I don't see how this could have gone worse, short of you

getting yourself an interview on Oprah to tell all. What the hell happened?"

"There was interference, Timothy. I was going for a clean single, and somehow that stupid bitch blundered right into my trajectory as I fired," she said. "I would have had him, but suddenly she was there, and I couldn't take back the shot."

"Instead of removing a minor sheik, Marjory, you sanctioned the U.S. Ambassador's wife. This has gotten very high profile. It's big in the news cycle. There are even rumors that this was a professional hit, not some act of terrorism. International sabres are being rattled."

"I realize this is a screw-up of epic proportions, but..."

"The board is very upset. Very. Upset. We live in the shadows, and you have shined the light very close to all of us."

"What are they saying, Timothy?"

"It's not that they give a damn about the woman herself, but her husband's position is keeping this in the limelight," he said. "Congressional fishing expeditions, three-letter agency investigations, and of course, a thousand conspiracy theories on social media networks. Some of those are actually a little too close to the truth. We've had to use our own technical resources to put forward and push alternative narratives."

"The bottom line?"

"The board thinks that you are incompetent, which is the other big concern here. An incompetent operator is dangerous to our organization, and it would take a great deal, an impressive demonstration to make them think otherwise."

Timothy had just thrown her a bone. Maybe she wasn't quite dead yet.

"So what you seem to be saying is that I might be able to redeem myself."

"Call it a demonstration of proficiency," he said. "An operation you would have to provide a target for and finance yourself."

She moved through her mental filing system and a light bulb came on. "There might be something, but the... mark is pretty low-profile."

"That would actually be for the best, considering. You would, of course, have to document everything in meticulous detail, and it would have to be done strategically. Simply plowing someone off a motorcycle or shooting them through their front door is not going to impress anyone. It must be a campaign, intelligently pre-planned. A show of mere lethality isn't going to cut it. We already know you can kill efficiently."

"Then, I'm to be given a chance? This job, it's been on my back burner for a couple of years." She saw his eyebrow raise, and hastily continued, "Really, Timothy. It was a job that I could have taken anytime, but the Association was keeping me busy with better paying work. As I said, the target isn't high profile..."

"This will need to be creative, my dear. I have gone out on a limb to get you this chance, and as I said, You will have to document the entire affair very meticulously. And again, you will have to finance the entire thing. This is less about the kill, than to prove that you have the three-dimensional thinking and care to pull off a job with consummate skill."

"I can do that for this job, Timothy. Can you convince them to let me try?"

The faintest hint of a smile tugged at his mouth. "Merry Christmas, Marjory. In September. I wish to make myself clear though, if you fuck up, I'd run far and fast to someplace remote. You'll be part of the Association's current to-do list if this doesn't work out."

2

"We're almost there, Mac!" Rosa's voice came back over her shoulder.

Since I knew the area we were running through like the back of my hand, I didn't comment. I was feeling pretty content though. Rosa Fernandez and I had just completed an eighteen mile (round trip) run through the Colockum Wildlife Refuge, moving over the old farm roads that wound through certain parts of that large wilderness preserve.

My contentment wasn't just coming from our having run that far. It was also coming from the fact that we weren't exhausted. Not even close.

The two of us were in training for an ultra-mountain marathon race through the Cascade mountains, which would be a lot longer than eighteen miles, but still, we'd run far, we'd run fast, and we were still doing just fine. Take your contentment where you can get it.

We started down the switchback road to my home, and greatly slowed our pace on the smashed basalt that paves the way down to my trailer.

I live on one of the more beautiful sections of the

Columbia River, adjacent to the Colockum Wildlife Refuge. My little old Airstream trailer sits near the base of an impressive basalt cliff, and a small stream runs right by the trailer.

Being far from most of the other homes along the Malaga highway, there's a lot of wildlife, everything from deer to beaver, with even the occasional bear wandering through. Two years ago, I watched a rare moose grazing on the water plants at the edge of the river, which is a little weird considering I live in what's technically classified as desert.

"Home sweet home," Rosa said as we slowed to a walk. "First dibs on the shower."

"Gah! You always say that, Rosa. Guess I'll just sit out here on the porch and air dry."

"Sorry you don't have a larger water heater, but... well... not my problem, is it? I just speak up faster, so I get the warm water."

"You're right," I said, "who can compete with the fast tongue of The Fernandez? Maybe while you're using my tiny shower, I'll go down to the south end of the property and check the haunted houses."

Two very old houses (and I use the term loosely) sit moldering along the river at the east end of my land, and I'm afraid that some wandering hiker might go into them someday and get hurt. People sue over just about anything these days. My Uncle Gil has advised me to make sure they don't need to be demolished completely.

"No, no, no," Rosa replied, "if these derelicts are as bad as your Uncle Gil has said, I want to be there with you. Don't go into them without me being there. Sabé?"

"Okay, if it'll ease your mind. Maybe I'll go down and take a dip in the river. Wash the first layer of sweat off until my water heater can get its venerable act together."

"You macho bahstid," Rosa said. "This late in the year, you won't see me getting in that river. I hate freezing."

"Believe me, I won't be in there long. Still, it's not like the cold of spring time. Just pretty invigorating."

"As you wish. Just don't drown. Imma go shower now." She went into the Airstream, I headed toward the Columbia River, surveying the view to the other side.

Development is starting to happen across the river. the onset of riverside "estates" starting to replace the sagebrush over there. But on my side, there's no place for a money-hungry real estate investor to get any purchase on the land. My mom and I occupy the last bits of habitable land at the end of the road, she in a ranch-style near the end of the high-way, and me in the trailer at the end the dirt road.

Rosa hadn't been that far off about the water temperature. While it didn't have the icy "just coming off the mountain snows" bite of springtime, it was still pretty damn chill wading out in just my running shorts.

Coming back to my porch, I picked up my sweatshirt, a ratty faded blue thing that reads, in faint letters, "I put the fun in dysfunctional," and used it to towel off. I'd take a real shower later, once my elderly water heater provided enough of the good stuff to do so.

A few minutes later, Rosa emerged from the Airstream in her civilian (non-running) clothes, looking gorgeous as always. She couldn't help it. She's a five-foot-ten inch, long-lashed, full-lipped, body of a human tigress, bombshell. I still get a little light-headed when she kisses me.

"Tomorrow's the day," she said. "We're going to try to run for a very long time while trying to stay on a mountain trail. Are we up for it, *Cariño?*"

"I sure hope so," I replied. "I know the old native runners of some of the tribes could do it, but they lived their entire lives running from here to there. We're in better shape than most humans on the planet, but I'm not sure that's saying a lot, surveying the general population. But the longest run we've done was still twenty miles less than the course for tomorrow. That has me worried."

"There's nothing more we can do, Mac. Sandra even said that this marathon was just something to try to finish. If our running mentors are willing to tell us something like that, they're quietly saying we don't have a chance to win. This race is a stepping stone to getting better at farther and faster."

"That's funny. Her husband Dave made noises like he thinks we can place in the race. Kinda mixed messaging there."

"Well, I'm not gonna let that intimidate me. Let's do some stretching and then we can go see about your "haunted houses," okay?"

———

Standing at the farthest down-river edge of my property, we surveyed my kingdom's slum section. The two old 1920's era houses that I needed to check out were on a spit of land that extended into the river. Normally rife with willows and European blackberries, there were occasional flood years where the entire tiny peninsula was under water. As were the foundations of the broken-down houses.

The first house was sinking in on itself in a huge patch of blackberries, one of the few I'd seen that were this large on the east side of the Cascade mountains. Next summer I'd have quite a harvest, but now, the thorny, berry-less vines wouldn't allow access to the old house without a lot of work. From what I could see of the mostly collapsed building, it wasn't worth the investment of time and sweat. No one but a complete masochist would try to enter the collapsed wreck of a structure.

"This barely qualifies as a structure anymore," Rosa said.

"You couldn't pay me to try and crawl in there through those thorns."

"Well, let's take a look at *numero dos*, then." I said to myself, walking farther toward the water.

The second house was in better shape, better being a relative term. The roof, while there, was sagging, holed, and would undoubtedly not even keep out a light rain. The windows were long gone, and I could see inside through the drooping front door sill that the entrance and floor within were covered with river sand from flooding not too many years past. It made me glad my beloved Airstream was higher up, nearer the cliffs. The dams above would have to completely collapse for the river to get there.

"Looks like there might be a basement," Rosa said, pointing at a sunken area in which a remaining intact window pane peeked out of the sand.

The old house was built from cinder blocks, for sturdiness and at the time, probably because they were cheap. There were a couple gaps in the walls and foundation, but they were small ones. Concrete blocks tend to last. The foundation itself looked like a combination of concrete and basalt rock. The sizable collapsed section had quite a lot of snapped off rebar sticking out.

"Looks like this part of the basement wall collapsed," I said, looking at a section on the side of the house perpendicular to the front door. "That alone is probably my answer about getting this place demolished."

I stuck my head in the front door, assessing the state of the ceiling. It looked sound enough, other than a few holes here and there. I decided to step in.

I had barely moved in a yard, putting all my weight on the sand-covered floor, when I had a sensation of falling. I heard wood rending and cracking and from pure reaction threw myself as far forward as I could. I landed on another section of floor farther ahead, and waited for the whole thing to collapse, but luck was with me. There was no give in the section I was crawling on.

It sounds crazy, but I looked back at the section of floor that I'd escaped from and it almost looked like it raised a little, moving back into place now that there was no weight on it. Only a skilled observer would notice the slight rearrangement of the sand that lay on top of it.

Haunted house? Death trap from hell?

"Mac? What happened?"

"Don't try to come in, Rosa! The floor in front of the door almost collapsed underneath me. See if you can get around to the back."

I very gingerly made my way forward, testing every step, but there were no more weak boards. I made my way around a concrete and brick wall, that most likely was functioning as the main support for the house, and transitioned from sand-covered wood to sand-covered concrete flooring.

The wall, at the end I'd come around formed a concrete "T" where it intersected with the primary wall. In the corner on the far side of the room sat the rusting remains of what had probably been a very fine cast iron kitchen stove. The rest of the kitchen was bare, having been long ago picked clean by time and scavengers. The only thing remaining besides the rusted hulk of the stove was the rusted lid of an old enameled coffee pot.

I stepped out the doorless rear entrance, noting that the foundation was crumbling in several places. Rosa was there.

"What happened in there, Mac? One second you were entering the front door, the next you looked like you'd taken flight."

"The damn floor started to go underneath me. I jumped just in time, and here's the weird part, when I was off it, it almost looked like it moved back into place."

She looked at me for a moment and her skepticism was palpable. "Let's see if we can get a look into the basement. I'd like to see this haunted doorway from below."

Looking around, I saw a cellar door on the side of the house. It gaped like a black hole and obviously went down to the basement level. I carefully took a look inside, and brushing away spider webs with a stick, I entered, not going in too deeply.

It wasn't as dark as I had expected it to be. The hole in the foundation near the door let in a fair amount of light. Even though it was a deep basement, parts of it were half filled with sand. Where there was no sand, crumbled sections of broken concrete and rebar littered the place. Toward the front door area, the basement floor dipped deeply, I guessed perhaps rutted out by flood waters. I was chilled to see the pile of broken rebar and concrete in that area, the area I had almost fallen through. Several shards of rebar stood almost straight up like spears. The broken concrete could easily break your back if you landed on it.

That's a trap worthy of the Viet Cong.

My mentor Ed, now in his mid-seventies, had told me stories of the horrific traps that the enemy during that particular war had used. This pile of sharp points was in just the right spot, and I was sure if I'd been alone and fallen through, it might have been a long time before my body would have been found.

"Yeah, I'm thinking you definitely need to get this place demolished," Rosa said. She'd crept in behind me and was surveying the death trap with the same trepidation on her face that I was feeling. "I'm really glad you didn't go through that floor."

"You and me both."

We turned and made our way out, and I found that the willows on this side of the house made it difficult to get back out to the road. There was however, no way I was going to go back through the house.

I'd have to do something about this dangerous 'nuisance,' but it would have to be later. Demolition looked like it would need to be conducted by professionals. In the meantime, I'd need to remember to draw up a sign to tell the curious to stay the eff out.

3

The neighborhood was quiet at 2:00 a.m., but surveillance cameras never sleep.

Unless of course they were blanked out remotely.

She'd taken her time, staying back in the shadows until she'd identified the two cameras overlooking her point of contact. Then, aiming her device at each in turn, she fried their circuits. It wasn't as elegant as looping footage, but it had the plausible deniability of equipment failure. Since both cameras were linked, it'd look like a power surge had blown them out.

She carried a small canvas backpack over one shoulder, just tall enough to conceal the prybar she assumed she'd need to complete the retrieval. Her mission hadn't really seemed like it would need her long-dead client's money to finish such a piece of cake job as killing MacKenzie Crow.

She'd planned to get it eventually though, no point in leaving money on the table. Or in the wall. She'd removed fifty grand from her own accounts the week before, for operating and life expenses, and that should easily cover costs with a large amount to spare. Her client's money was simply her reward for doing the job. Or if things didn't pan out and she had to run.

There was a snag to her plan, though. The client's money <u>*had*</u> *become important because the Council had frozen her accounts.*

She hadn't known the bastards could do that. A little research led her to conclude that the Association, through many shell corporations, had a controlling stock in the institution where they'd set up an account for her. Her thoughts, for a moment, had turned to revenge, but trying to fight back against the Association would be a quick ticket to the long dirt nap.

She'd gone through the stages of loss before coming up with a plan for her survival and, going cold, started to use her head. With the money Dallum had left for his petty little hit, and the money she'd withdrawn, she could get by. She'd plan out her campaign, off the kid, and then be re-admitted to the Association.

"That'd better be what happens, or I might need to disappear completely."

Obviously not everyone on the Council had her best interests at heart. Some of them wanted her to fail, as much a swipe at her mentor Timothy, as a punitive measure directed toward herself. Pettiness could infect the most professional of organizations, and some of her contemporaries had egos the size of the moon.

Now she <u>*needed*</u> *Dallum's hidden money, even though coming here was notably out of her way, and was taking valuable time she couldn't afford to waste.*

Nonetheless, no mission was successful without sufficient funding.

Marjory moved to a shadowy area of the street, a spot where the light from street lamps didn't quite meet, and crossed the street. Reaching the eight-foot-high brick wall of the now shuttered mansion, its fate tied down in multiple probate-based lawsuits, she began counting bricks to the left of the large main gate. There was still a security guard in the small booth there, but he was mind-locked into the phone in his left hand. His right hand was in his front pants pocket, and was moving furiously under the cloth. She'd have to make a major ruckus to get him to look up and do his job. She continued counting.

Reaching brick ten from the gate and six up, she aimed her tiny tactical flashlight at the corner of it. In a tiny relief on the lower left corner was the image of a lion.

Just like the old man had said when he'd originally tried to recruit her.

Wrapping a soldier's shemaugh scarf around the end of the prybar, she jammed the tip between the bricks. It took three strikes to get into the mortar far enough to begin to pry, each one making her glance toward the gate, but the security guard was oblivious. Hell, he hadn't even noticed that some of his cameras were non-functional.

Marjory pried, making sure not to make any huge breaks, ready to snatch any large debris before it hit the ground. With a snap, the brick split and before a section of it could fall she had it in hand, placing it gently on the sidewalk.

Shining her light on the hole she'd made, she saw the corner of what could only be a freezer bag.

The money was here. Time to move on to the assassination of one MacKenzie Crow.

4

I think she's trying to kill me.

I looked up the long trail we'd been running on for most of the day at the muscular back of my partner, Rosa. Tough as she is, I could see she was starting to fade. She may be the love of my life, but talking me into running a huge trail marathon through the back country made me wonder if she'd taken out a six-figure insurance policy on me.

As if telepathically feeling my eyes on her, she looked back. Through ragged breaths she said, "Hang in there, Mac. We've passed the three quarters mark."

Which was great, but I was starting to feel my body give out protests I couldn't ignore anymore. In my capacity as junior member of a bounty hunting team, led by my Uncle Gil, I had taken some fairly serious physical damage a while back. A year and a half ago, a sociopathic bastard had slashed me with a machete in the leg and across the chest, leaving some epic warrior scars. The largest was a scar that went from one side of my chest to the other. The second scar was across an older scar on the outside of my left thigh, and the combination of the two gave me a strange "X" on that leg.

"I'm hanging'... in... there," I managed to gasp out in response. The truth was, I was pretty sure that something was going wrong in the healed cuts, even after all this time. Aside from the mounting ache, I kept feeling a sensation of dampness where the ache in my thigh was. I glanced down, but I didn't see anything, though trying to do a self exam while running over a rocky trail was high on the difficulty scale.

This marathon was different from most. It was a team event, in groups of four, and it was required that the entire team finish. The last person in the team dictated the team's final finish time.

A recipe for disaster in our case.

I don't know what possessed Dave Wessel and his wife Sandra to invite Rosa and I to be the second part of their team. The two of them had been doing marathons for years, both of them in their late thirties, whereas I had been trail-running with Rosa for less than a year. They both had been very encouraging, practicing with us, pushing us forward in our distances, but they knew we were inexperienced in something this long. Sandra had even said so.

Dave was an upper level manager at AltMed-Tech, which, as the name implies, is a medical technology design company. He was used to being in charge of people. He was smooth when it came to managing the troops.

Until the actual race, that is.

The honeymoon was over at the first rest and rehydration stop.

"What the hell are you wearing?" Dave asked me as we stood, rehydrating the copious amounts of water we'd sweated out in the first mountainous stretch. He pointed at the tiny waist pack I had around my waist.

"It's an emergency kit, but it only weighs six ounces." I

replied. "It's just for emergencies or if for some reason, we get stuck out here."

He put his palms over his face for a moment and rubbed down. "Every ounce slows you down, and slows the team down, Mac."

"We're going out pretty far in these mountains, Dave. I kinda like to have at least a small bit of preparedness on me."

"Mac, there are checkpoints every ten miles. There's nothing in this that you need to be prepared for other than putting one foot in front of the other as fast as you can. Please," he said, voice slightly rising, "go hand that shit off to one of the volunteers and get your head in the game."

Occasionally, I go against my better judgement at the behest of older and 'wiser' heads, and it almost always winds up biting me in the ass. He turned away, and I headed toward the volunteers, but as soon as he wasn't looking at me, I put the tiny waist pack back on under my untucked running shirt, covering my kit with my shirt tail. Dave hadn't noticed the paracord bracelet with its tiny blade, compass and ferro rod, so I also kept those, pretty sure that the two ounces it represented weren't going to make a difference in where we finished in the race.

As I stood, drinking electrolyte-laced water, Rosa came over to me. "Is it just me, or is Dave starting to go from Dr. Jekyll to Mr. Hyde?"

"I guess this race means a lot to him."

"Yeah. Looks like Sandra's about to catch some of his ultra competitive bullshit now." We watched as Dave started yelling at his wife, occasionally gesturing our way. Sandra's expression, as she tried to talk sanity to him started getting more and more mask-like, never a good sign when talking to one's love interest. Finally, she motioned to Rosa and I, pointed at the trail and took off.

Dave stood there a moment, watching her with a surprised expression, then started following her.

"Guess that's our cue," Rosa said.

"Yep." We started after them.

That seemed like it had happened days ago.

We were now three quarters through the race and had no reserves left. I was distracting myself by watching my team's tracks in the dusty trail, which if you're not a tracker, as I am, is probably a pretty odd-sounding thing to do. I could easily make out Rosa's Brook Cascadias, since she was only about fifty yards ahead of me. I was also very familiar with the Scarpa Neutron's that Dave and Sandra were wearing. I'd been watching Dave's large prints and Sandra's more petite ones since the first stop, gauging how far ahead they were by the degradation of their tracks in the dust and by how many other racers had stepped on their tracks.

I love being in nature, it is the balm to my soul. But being in nature, and being in pain? Not quite the same level of enjoyment. It's said, in the nineteenth and early twentieth centuries, there were numerous records of Native American runners traveling hundreds of miles over broken country in a few short days, little worse for wear. I obviously was not able to measure up to that. Yet.

Rosa and I were in a race filled with world-class athletes, and if Dave hadn't pulled some sort of strings that I didn't have a clue about, we very likely wouldn't have qualified.

"Mac! Another hydration stop ahead!" Rosa called back.

"Oh, thank God."

When we arrived at the resting area, Sandra and Dave were both there.

Dave was looking daggers at us. He once again turned to Sandra, pointing towards Rosa and I. He didn't even try to keep his voice down this time.

"You sure picked a couple of winners for the team, Sandra.

These two don't have the stamina my grandma has. We're not even going to place in the top fifteen teams."

"David," Sandra remarked. "They're new to this. You can't expect them to be world-class on their first long trail run. They'll get better. They'll learn more about how to conserve their resources with experience. You knew we wouldn't win this. This race is just a stepping stone."

"I had had to do some serious ass-kissing to get these two qualified. The least they could do," he raised his voice, "is put some effort into this!"

I had had enough and was about to blast him, when Rosa moved in front of me, and quietly facing him said, "David. This is not how you inspire the troops. Mac and I have been giving everything we have."

His expression changed briefly, and I think he realized he'd crossed the line but then, his face changed again, and even without being telepathic, I knew he'd just decided, "screw it."

"This was a mistake. The only reason Sandra even contacted you two was because we literally couldn't find anyone else to fill the two slots on the team. All we've accomplished is to ruin my reputation with all these people. Well, at least I can go ahead of you all and finish with the winners, even if my team can't. Sandra, let's go."

I was pissed. We'd already run quite a bit farther than most regular marathons, and that on mountain trails. He was making it sound like we'd just gotten off the couch after eating a box of Twinkies, while playing video games all day.

We'd given our all, and he was cutting us loose.

I wasn't the only one who was angry. I could see the tight line Rosa's lips had compressed to, but looking over to Sandra, I was almost surprised at the outrage on her face.

"Mac, Rosa, I am SO sorry. I've never seen him act like

this before," she said. She started up the trail, but there was little enthusiasm in her pace.

"I think I'm done," I said. "I just now, oddly enough, stopped giving a crap about this race."

Rosa turned to me, and I was surprised to see an almost pleading look on her face. "Mac, I know that we have zero incentive to finish it, but... we've run so far. I just really want to at least make it across the finish line. Not for Dave, but..."

No other human being on the planet could have induced me to run another step for this 'team' but looking down into those tired, trail-dusted, astonishingly beautiful eyes, I knew I'd keep going. Crawling over broken glass if necessary.

"For us," I replied. "Yeah. I feel more tired and sore than I ever have in my life, Rosa. But yeah, let's do this. I'm no damn quitter."

Rosa reached up and gave me a salty kiss. "I love men who don't quit."

"Really? Well... don't expect miracles for a day or two. Let's go."

We started up the trail, on the final section, a quarter of the race still to go. Each time we stopped it was that much harder to start up again, but the rest had at least allowed us to stop and do some deep breathing. Earlier, my muscles after the first two stops had stayed warm enough that the slight rest allowed me to pick up the pace again.

Not this time. My muscles were now informing me that they hated me, and promised revenge, horrible sadistic revenge, tomorrow.

Shortly thereafter, a pair of runners passed us, and even though we were, in essence, competitors, one of them gasped out, "Hang in there guys, final stretch!" which I thought was pretty nice, considering the encouragement we'd received from our own peerless leader.

I started once again to watch the tracks on the trail. It

was kind of a pity to roam through beautiful scenery mostly watching the ground, but I was trying to self-hypnotize. By watching and noting variations in the tracks, I was taking my mind off the increasing pain of my body.

"Mac," Rosa said from twenty feet ahead of me, "look who's coming back."

We'd run another seven miles from the last stop, but the last person I expected to see before the end was Dave Wessel. Dave came towards us at a light jog, and I could see in his face he didn't want to talk to us, but getting close, he had no choice.

"Have... either of you two seen Sandra? I wanted to... apologize. I thought I'd see her before now. Did you two pass her?" The skepticism in that question started to raise my hackles again, but Rosa stepped forward and answered calmly.

"She was ahead of us. Are you sure she didn't pass you?" she said.

"No," he said with such derision that if I'd been able to lift my leg, I might've front-kicked him off the trail. "She hasn't passed me."

"If she hasn't passed you, and we haven't passed her, the only answer is that she left the trail." I said.

"Where? Where would she do that?" he said. "There's no real trails off-shooting the main one in this area. And why would she?"

I had a pretty good idea why, and so did Rosa. She gave me a subtle look as I started to say why, shaking her head ever so slightly, and I bit back some angry words. She was right. Figuring out where our missing team member went was the main issue here. Recriminations would just muddy the water.

"Mac," Rosa said. "Do you see her tracks?"

I have been training rigorously to be a man-tracker for the last decade, and over that time I've developed a "library system" for my brain of the tracks I've seen. I began shuffling mental note cards. I remembered seeing Rosa's, Dave's and Sandra's tracks when we'd started out from the last stop but as I ran through, I realized I hadn't seen Sandra's in a while. It was a testament to how tired I was that I'd noted it subconsciously, but not on a conscious level.

"No, her tracks aren't here. Somewhere on the way, she detoured. Maybe a potty break and we passed her? Or maybe she's just pissed at you, Dave. One of us should go back to make sure she's coming, though." I wasn't keen in any way to re-cover the miles we'd just run, but I was starting to get the "oogie" feeling. That clenching in my gut was almost never wrong.

"I'll go," Dave said, and started back the way we'd all come.

"Let's head for the finish line, Mac." Rosa turned the way we'd been going. She stopped when she saw I hadn't moved, that I was watching Dave recede down the trail. "Mac?"

"We need to follow him."

"Why?"

I sighed. "I... I have a bad feeling..."

She looked at me. "Alright. Your hunches have saved our asses on more than one occasion. Let's..." It was her turn to sigh, "..go back."

We started after Dave.

None of us were running too hard, and other competitors met us running the other way. Without exception, they gave us strange looks, and a few mentioned the actual direction of the finish line. Rosa told them we had a missing team-mate.

It was two miles back, when I noticed Sandra's tracks again, running the opposite direction. They were harder to see, having been tromped on by other competitors, but it only took one clear print, and I knew it was her.

"She was still heading toward the finish line at this point," I said, pointing at the track. "We need to turn around."

"How do you know?" Dave said.

"TRACKER!" I said, jerking a thumb in my own direction. "Pay attention."

Rosa looked at me, and I realized just how angry that had sounded.

So... damn tired.

Heading back toward the finish line again, for some reason Sandra's tracks became easier to see. They almost had a slight glow to them. I had an idea what that was, and when you are that tired, you'll take anything you can get. We'd gone barely a hundred yards when I noticed a faint game trail leading off the main course. There was a fresh scuff mark where it started down. I took a few steps down, and just past some roots, I found a clear track.

Sandra's.

"This way. She's down here."

"Why the hell did she go down there?" Dave asked. "It's barely a trail."

"You can ask her when we find her," Rosa said.

5

It was at least a quarter mile, through a trail that faded in and out, before I heard the sobbing. I was moving in a criss-cross pattern, trying to stay with the vanishing trail, when I saw a flash of bright lime green and orange. I started moving toward the out-of-place color.

"Sandra!" Dave yelled out. "Where are you?"

"Here!" A ragged voice replied, the sound coming from the spot I was heading. A few dozen more steps, and I could see Sandra in a perplexing position. She was face down in the trail, her legs lying across a small log with her feet elevated, and she didn't look very comfortable. I was about to ask her if she was injured when I saw the blood pooling under the log.

"Sandra! Honey, what's wrong?" Dave cried out.

"I'm stuck... there's... a piece of this log in my leg. Ahhhh! It hurts!"

"Jeez. She's got a broken off branch from this thing stuck in her quad," Rosa said as she kneeled and looked under our team mate. "She's pinned to it. Steady stream of blood leaking out."

"Ahhh God, I feel so stupid," Sandra sobbed. "I'm so sorry."

"Baby, don't worry," Dave said. "We'll get you out of this." He'd dashed to her and obviously having no idea what to do, began lightly patting her back. He looked back at us hopefully.

We all have a dirty little nasty part of ourselves that wants to kick someone when they're down, and Dave Wessel's earlier behavior made it a real fight for my better self to not be an utter a-hole. But I choked back a bitter remark and looked at Rosa. She'd seen combat in the Middle East, and I wanted her to take the lead on this. Unsurprisingly, she was up for the challenge.

"All right, boys, let's focus," "Dave," Rosa said. "You lift her legs. I'll get under her ribs and Mac will lift at her hips. We get her up, and take her over to that grassy spot over there and set her down. We can apply what first aid we can then and someone can go for help."

"Let's do it," I said. "Sandra, this is gonna be rough..."

"Just do it!" she sobbed.

So we did. Each of us got our arms under Sandra, and on Rosa's count of three we lifted simultaneously. There was a squelching sound as Sandra came free of the log that turned my stomach, but that was nothing compared to the screech the victim let out.

"Ahhhhh! Jesus!! OH!!!"

We carried her the ten yards to the grass, and gently set her down in a sitting position. Blood was oozing from the wound, and that in itself was probably irrigating out small bits of flotsam from the wound, but we had to stop the flow.

"Mac, I see you still have that little kit with you," Rosa said. "What've we got to work with besides sweaty clothing?"

"The stuff in my first aid kit is too small to deal with something this big, but I have a bandana, and a spool of dental floss for cordage. If we had water bottles we could irrigate the wound, but..."

"First priority is to get that wound as plugged up as best we can," Rosa said. "The bandana will make a decent covering, but we don't have anything to clot the wound with."

"There's Usnea hanging on all these trees," I said. They both looked at me like I had lost my mind.

"You want to use that hanging moss in her wound? What the hell..?" Dave blurted out.

"Usnea has potent antibacterials that helps prevent wounds from getting infected," I told him. "A little, folded to slow down blood flow, and the bandana on top of it might get her stable enough we can go for help. There's most likely gonna be fragments of the branch in there anyway, and that's just too much for us to irrigate out, even if we had water."

Rosa covered the wound with my bandana, but it was obvious it was going to saturate quickly. I dashed around the clearing, grabbing as much hanging moss off the trees as quickly as I could. When I had enough. Rosa lifted the bandana and helped me pack a wadding of moss over the wound. Then we tied the bandana back in place with dental floss. Dental floss is strong stuff, and I use it for cordage in all my kits. When we were done, the bleeding seemed to be stopped. Or at least slowed a great deal.

"I hope we're doing the right things with that moss," Rosa said.

"She's already lost a lot of blood, and the bandana wasn't stopping the blood loss well enough. Fingers crossed. Now, someone's got to get back to the last waypoint and bring back the first responders they had there."

We both looked at Dave.

"Me?" he said. "I think I should stay with Sandy..."

"You were just telling us that you're the fastest, and you still have energy to burn, so use that to go and get help," Rosa told him. The Marine Corps authority in her voice got him off his butt and heading up the trail.

"And when you get to the main trail," I yelled after him, "make sure you mark the way down here so you can find us again."

Dave looked back at us and headed up the way we had come.

———

It was about an hour and a half before anyone came to help. Rosa and I sat with Sandra, trying to distract her from the pain she was in. Because of the spartan nature of the race, we had very little in the way of aid supplies, and certainly no pain killers.

"I feel so stupid. Talk about idiot gestures," she said.

"You did this for Dave, right?" Rosa asked.

"Not so much... for Dave. More to kick him in the head to loosen up some of the rocks in there. I'd just had enough. I know my actions weren't logical but I reached my breaking point. I couldn't take it anymore. Dave gets tyrannical in a competition, and I was sick of it," she said, leaning her head back against a stump. "It's like he turns into another person entirely."

"Sandra, are you safe?" Rosa asked. "Is Dave violent?"

Sandra shook her head. "No. He would never hurt me. Except with his words."

"Emotional abuse is still abuse," Rosa objected.

"Yes, but it's only when it comes to competitions. Otherwise he is fine to be around."

I could see that Rosa thought there might be a better way to have a conversation with Dave about his actions than getting lost in the woods, and no doubt that was occurring to Sandra now as well. Better left unsaid.

"Competitions just seem to make him a little crazy." Sandra told us.

"So we saw," I said. Rosa gave me a hard look.

"I am so sorry," Sandra said, more tears starting to leak out. Rosa arched her eyebrows at me and gestured with her eyes toward our wounded team mate.

"Hey," I said. "Rosa and I are big kids now. Let's not sweat the small stuff. Wish they'd hurry up and get here though. What do you want to bet you're gonna get to ride in a helicopter."

"Oh, that'll be fun," Sandra said with little enthusiasm.

"Plus some really great painkillers."

"That I can get behind," she said with a pained laugh.

We heard dry limbs and twigs snapping above us, and standing up, I saw Dave and two other men carrying small packs with visible medical symbols on their exteriors. The cavalry was here.

Rosa and I stepped back as the First Responders went to work. One of the men talked on a satellite phone while looking at his GPS. We watched as they worked and Dave finally came over to us, looking sheepish.

"Guys, I'm... I'm sorry about what I said earlier," he said. "I was a true jackass. I'm... just.. sorry."

There is a time for snark and a time for kindness. I remembered the poster on the wall of my mom's tiny office at the hospital back home. *You have no idea the battles that people are fighting. Whenever possible, just be kind.* I sighed.

"Forget about it, man, that's all past. What's important is Sandra. Are they bringing in a chopper?"

"Yeah. The first aid guys say that we'll need to get her down to that small meadow over there. They're gonna rig some type of sling chair so we can work as a team."

Within a half hour, we were carrying Sandra the two hundred yards to the meadow. Dave was on her upper left side and I was on the upper right. The two responders carried Sandra near her lower torso. Rosa went ahead and pushed brush aside so we could get through. Normally, it wouldn't have been that much of a strain, but Dave and I were both tired as hell and the short distance down seemed like miles.

Sandra was wrapped in an emergency blanket, and she groaned when we set her down. She looked pale and tired and I was extremely glad when I heard the helicopter, most likely from Harborview in Seattle, flying up the canyon. The chopper never actually landed, but rigged a stretcher on a winch and raised her up into the bird that way. Then they brought Dave up in a sling seat so he could fly with her. Five minutes later, it was just Rosa, myself and the emergency medical guys.

We started the long walk back up the hill.

―――――

When we finally emerged at the end of the race, all of the other competitors were long gone. Rosa and I were hobbling, but we were still going. In comparison, the two EMTs were looking like rock stars. Much to our surprise, aside from a few remaining race officials waiting to make sure everyone was in, there were also a few reporters, and assorted people taking photos of us.

I was sure I had never been this tired before, not even when Rosa and I had needed to fight our way out of the North Cascades during a winter storm. I tilted my head up to the sky, eyes closed and just breathed in the cool evening air.

Through my eyelids I could see more camera flashes, but I didn't care. Normally Rosa and I and all our associates, being bounty hunters, try to avoid being in the limelight, but we were so tired, it just didn't matter. No doubt we would be so grungy and disheveled we'd be unrecognizable anyway.

"Well, looks like you two finally crossed the finish line," a gravelly voice said.

"Hey Uncle Gil. Thanks for coming to pick us up." I said to my craggy-faced mentor and employer. "Guess our time wasn't too impressive, hunh?"

"Maybe not, if you're fool enough to compare yourselves to the pros, but if you simply note that you ran seventy-five miles through the backcountry and saved a woman's life, I'd say it was pretty damn good." He looked at Rosa. "So, you up for hunting a bounty tomorrow, Ms. Fernandez?"

"Tomorrow?" Rosa and I said simultaneously, not even attempting to keep the whine out of our voices.

"A local official, having been caught red-handed embezzling from county funds, skipped his court date and has disappeared. The gentleman has family up in Okanogan county, near Oroville, as well as a nice vacation home on a fairly remote mountain lake. Thought we'd just go see if he was dumb enough to go there. Tomorrow."

"Mac and I'll be moving like octogenarians tomorrow," Rosa told him. "Can we at least wait until afternoon? I don't think you'll be able to raise me outta bed before ten a.m., Gilbert."

"Not a problem, he shouldn't have any idea we're coming. We'll meet at the office about two p.m., if you two seniors can make it in."

"We'll make it," I said. "But don't expect us to be fast."

6

"Wenatchee is one of those little cities just barely big enough to have a freakin' Costco," she said into the tiny recorder. "It's kind of pretty, though the hills around here are a uniform brown. I guess that's a fall thing."

She was sitting on a bench under some sort of leafy tree that was just starting to turn color. The bench was several yards from the paved trail that meandered along the waterfront.

"Seems to be a gun lovin' city. I've seen a lot of pick-ups with visible guns in the back and bumper stickers mentioning 'cold dead fingers.' Not to mention a ton of churches and tattoo parlors. Obviously an identity problem. Anti-abortion billboards and vegan new-age health food stores. The whole damn city is in a river valley, with one major roadway down the center, withg a bridge at the north and south ends. Could be a problem if a fast getaway is needed. Roads are often congested. You almost have to be a local to know your way around."

Marjory paused the recorder for a moment. She thoughtfully gazed out over the sluggishly moving river, its momentum slowed by a dam miles farther down. A pair of joggers passed by on the manicured trail, and she waited until they were out of earshot before continuing.

"This place doesn't have a lot of big businesses, so income disparity shows in the houses. Either very nice houses or apartments or old motorhomes parked on the streets. Quite a number of homeless for such a dinky community."

She paused again, this time not for passersby, but to consider what she was saying. Was it of any importance? She sighed. Best to be thorough.

"The police department is right off the center of town, but the police don't have much of a presence, probably understaffed. Good sign. Wenatchee has a crime rate that is higher than 74% of Washington state's cities. The big river, the Columbia, that runs through it is a good thing. Big enough water that it'd be easy to dump a well-weighted body into, if needed."

She trailed off. That was probably more than enough detail about this podunk place. Time to get to the meat of the matter.

"I got a first look at my quarry yesterday up at a place called Stevens Pass, a mountain pass that's on one of the few major routes to actual civilization in Western Washington. Young MacKenzie Crow evidently is some sort of marathoner, if not a very good one. He was in the company of a tough-looking, but admittedly pretty woman named Rosa. From the documentary on the Survival show that went wrong, I gleaned that her full name is Rosa Fernandez. I have my Dark Web contact learning everything possible about her in addition to young Mac. Normally, the Association would be paying his search fees, but now it's all coming out of my pocket. I had no idea how much these hacker bastards cost."

She stopped and waited for another pair of early-morning runners to move past, and by ingrained reflex, cataloged the quickest kill-points on each before continuing. *"I also saw some of Mac's other support group members. Someone named 'Uncle Gil' and another named 'Vinn,' both of whom looked like tough customers. More research required."*

The sun was just starting to rise across the river and the reflection *was blinding. Marjory rose and started walking south along the riverfront and its abundant park areas.*

"I need to learn more about MacKenzie and his crew before I start planning my campaign," she said into the device. "I chose this mission because I once was tricked into saying I'd kill this young man by one of our former clients. I intend to show my skills at both planning and execution so that I may be reinstated. It would be almost no challenge at all to simply snipe him or walk up and stick a shiv into someplace rapidly lethal. People don't keep a close eye on their food when they're out and about. I could do any of these things and scoot, but that would impress no one. Any Pro-Am could do that."

She paused as an older man passed her, small white poof ball of a dog leashed to one hand, a small plastic bag of dog poo in the other. The man was diligently looking for a trash can. Marjory shuddered at the sight. Pets were for 'civilians' and the soft-hearted. She was neither.

Speaking into the recorder once again, she was cognizant of the fact that this record wasn't for her, but for the people that would judge her performance.

"For now, I'm going to sit back, bide my time and research my prey. After that, the plan I formulate will be the best way to make this poor dumb kid wish he'd never been born. That is what I was contracted for, and that's what will happen."

7

Things were just as I expected.

Every time Rosa and I increased our mileage, the next day would pay us back hard. Having gone through the penultimate mileage increase of our running journey, the muscular payback was equally epic.

We were in Rosa's RAV, me driving, and my mom riding shotgun. In the rear view mirror, I could see Rosa slumped back in her seat, a slight buzz of snoring emanating from her.

Lucky brat.

We were en route to Uncle Gil's farm, way on the other side of the Columbia River from my own home. For some reason, my uncle had decided on conducting our planning meeting at the farm, and he'd told me to bring Mom along.

To get to the farm, I had to drive twenty or so miles up the Malaga Highway to downtown Wenatchee. There we'd switched to Rosa's RAV from my Doom-Mobile pickup, and Rosa had informed me that I was driving. I was too tired to argue. (Though later, I realized I should've enlisted Mom to drive, then I could've been sawing logs in the passenger seat.)

We left Wenatchee, crossed the Sellars Bridge and turned

toward the Badger Mountain plateau which would take us to the dirt road leading to the farm. Uncle Gil liked his privacy.

"You two look like you've been beaten with a sack of door knobs," Mom said. "I'm so proud of you both for finishing, but that race was really too much."

"Heh. But think how good our butts are going to look. Not an ounce of fat left on either of us."

"You and Rosa were already as lean as starving wolves. Honestly, I think you were burning up your own muscles. I'm impressed either of you were able to get out of bed today."

"You're not the only one," Rosa's tired voice came from the back. "But when his highness, Gilberto Chambers the First, commands our presence, all we can do is appear and genuflect in his direction."

"God," I said, "I pray he's not serious about going after that yahoo politician today. I swear, all I'll be able to do is whisper encouragement to Vinnie and him from the car window."

"Yeah," Rosa replied. "I think if we're going today, you can be driver and I'll be navigator. Vinn and Gil can do all the heavy lifting."

"I'm sure that'll go over well with my brother," Mom said. "Mac, there's the turn-off." I'd almost missed it in my tiredness and had to slam on the brakes.

I turned off on the semi-graveled side road and began the last leg to the farm. We were up high now, the winding road following the contours of the rolling hills. On occasion I saw glimpses of the Columbia River's deep gorge as we passed through fields of wheat and open grass rangelands.

At one spot, out in the sagebrush and under some large Ponderosa pine trees, I saw some older motor homes and a couple of vans and older SUVs, several with visible solar panels. I wondered what it was like, living the nomadic life, finding a nice campsite and just plunking down for as long as I wanted to stay.

The modern nomads had mostly checked out of the rat race, some of them in massive "everything but the kitchen sink" rigs, some living out of Honda Civics. No mortgages, no utilities to pay, only select possessions. Some of them were now nomads due to the economic circumstances of America's corporatocracy economy, some simply fed up with pursuing the less and less attainable American Dream and the rat race that financed it.

Due to some recent serious windfalls, I'd been able to pay eighty percent of the mortgage on my little riverside paradise, but I lived in Chelan County. Our county assessor, unbeknownst to the public, is actually part of a long lineage of vampires. Since simply drinking our blood publicly is so gauche, he gets his satisfaction from trying to drain property owners dry through taxation. Fortunately, I'm way outside of any city limits, which is the only thing that saves me.

I'm fortunate in that the only intact permanent structure on my property is the small stone shed behind my trailer. This kept the taxes low even though I was living on riverfront property. My mom has donated every part of her own holdings, except her house and barn area, to the wildlife refuge. She still uses them, but no longer has to pay taxes on them.

Every once in a while, the idea of wandering with little contribution to modern "society" is very appealing.

"Mac, there's Gilbert's driveway," Mom said, interrupting my reverie.

I took a left into the long driveway, slowing down greatly to avoid hitting anything dashing out of the sagebrush and to avoid throwing up a dust storm behind us. Ahead, I could see the farm, with all its many outbuildings. Behind it was something new.

"Wait a sec. Are those... grapevines? What happened to

the wheat field?" I asked. "I swear, it was just out here less than a month ago."

"The farmer that leases Gil's fields has now subleased to one of the jillions of local wineries that's sprung up," Mom told me. "Evidently our local wines are turning into quite the export, and the land around here is perfect for growing grapes, if irrigated."

"That's it," Rosa said from the back, "I'm going to have a sign made for the driveway that says 'Chateau D' Chambers.' I'd guess the next thing will be for Gil to appear in front of the house with a new fire-engine-red Lamborghini. Everyone remember to kiss his ring when we are allowed to approach His Eminence."

Laughing, we pulled the RAV up in front of the main house. The laughter quickly faded as we opened the doors and tried to stand up. I had to half-fall out of the Rav to get out the driver's side. Glancing over my shoulder, I saw my mom pulling Rosa out of the car and helping her to a standing position.

"Aii!" Rosa said. "This is horrible! I don't think I was this sore on my worst day at Marine Corps boot camp, and that was tough. Tough, tough, tough."

"Yeah," was all I could reply. I hobbled over to her and took her hand. Rosa and I began walking toward the front porch, moving like two old turtles. I glanced back at Mom, and she was doing everything she could not to laugh. The grin on her face was not helpful.

"It's not funny," I said, mildly peeved.

"Oh, it's pretty funny Grandpa. Now, maybe you'll remember how it feels the next time you give your uncle and I crap about our aches and pains."

"Oh Lord," A voice said from inside the porch screen door. Melinda, once a client, now family, came out and surveyed our decrepitude. "Let's get you two into the house and start you chugging a pitcher of water. We'll wash that lactic acid out of you."

"In the meantime, I really need some more Vitamin I," Rosa told her.

"In this household, we have a large stock of Ibuprofen, my dear young warriors. We'll get you moving again, though I fear that as bad as you feel today, tomorrow will be worse. You should both stay here tonight, and use the hot tub. Besides, we don't get to visit enough."

"I.. Uh.. didn't bring a swimsuit," I said.

"Me neither," Rosa told her. "But that hot tub sounds so good!"

"Oh, kids," Melinda laughed. "Didn't you know? This is a house of loose morals. Ed and I sit in there *au naturel* on a regular basis. No suits to dry out afterwards."

Rosa and I stood there, determinedly striving to keep the image of our seniors sitting in the hot water naked out of our minds. Fortunately, Melinda misread our expressions.

"No need to be shy. We'll be sure to give you plenty of privacy. You can sit out there, and there's so little light pollution the stars seem to be right in front of your eyes. You just have to be careful not to have an out of body experience, or fall asleep and breathe underwater."

"At this point, an out of body experience sounds really good," Rosa said. "I'm up for an astral trip to the Pleiades that lasts about a week."

"Yeah, me too," I said. "Hey Mel, where's everyone else? I saw Vinnie's Bronco parked by the bunkhouse. I figured they'd all be here ready to razz us for being late."

"The boys are playing with a new toy parked in the barn. You should go out and check on them."

Rosa and I, having walked around a bit, were starting to loosen up. Moving through the screened porch on the back side of the house, water in hand, we walked out to the huge barn that had come with the farm when Uncle Gil bought the place. Voices could be heard, and they didn't sound happy.

"I'm tellin' you Gil, you guys bought a pig in a poke. The engine for this thing, once you can take a look with the valve covers off, it's toast."

"We knew it was a long shot, Vinn. That's why something this big was so cheap. But putting in a new engine would still be cheaper than buying something new."

As Rosa and I turned the corner and looked into the big open space, we saw what the "new toy" was. Sitting there was a motorhome large enough to fly fighter jets off of. In front of it, with the massive hood braced up, was Vinnie, the other member of our bounty hunting team, Uncle Gil and Ed Burn-baum. The three of them had body language that said, "Now whadda we do?"

"Wow, boys. You getting ready for a Mars mission?" Rosa said. "That thing is huge! What the heck are you gonna do with it?"

"The plan was to do whatever engine work it needed," Uncle Gil said in his bass gravel voice. "Then Mel, Ed and I were gonna tour the nation."

"Tour the nation?" I said, "What about your business?" What I was really asking was *"What about our source of income?"*

"If you can believe it, Mac," Vinnie said. "Ol' Gil here was going to rent us out."

"Thanks, Vinn. I couldn't have phrased that worse if I'd worked on that sentence for a week," Uncle Gil said with a dry tone. "The plan was eventually for us old fogies to take a six-month leave of absence and Tim Marano would provide you three with jobs until we got back. Ed, Mel and I are no spring chickens any more, and we want to see the country a bit. That plan, unfortunately, is on hold until we can source an engine for this thing."

Tim Marano was the man who'd gotten Uncle Gil into the

biz. He was a good friend of my uncle's and had a fair-sized bounty hunting business on the west side in Seattle.

"Does the rest of it work?" Rosa asked. Evidently being subcontracted out didn't bother her at all.

"Everything else works like a charm," Ed Burnbaum, the man who'd mentored me in tracking and survival said. Ed was a Viet Nam Special Forces veteran who'd spent a good portion of his civilian life living in a cabin hidden way out in the mountains. He'd helped a teenager with a love for the woods become a skilled tracker and primitive skills expert. "Hell, Gil. If nothing else, we could rent the thing out as an apartment."

"Actually, Ed. There's no one who's not currently on this property that I'd want living out here with us. I have zero interest in having strangers around."

"Well, then everyone come in for the celebration," Mom said, walking up behind us to see the huge boondoggle, "you can worry about your dead dinosaur later."

8

"The ease with which this mission could be accomplished is astonishing," she said into the recorder. "Target Crow lives in a remote trailer along the Columbia River. The nearest house is half a mile back down a dirt lane and he literally lives at the end of the world. I am currently sitting on a cliff right above his place and, if he were here, could snipe him at will." She switched the device off.

As Marjory surveyed the area, a number of scenarios came to mind for the elimination of young MacKenzie. She could literally toss a satchel of C4 the hundred feet to the top of his trailer and detonate it. She could lay a booby trap along the switchbacked gravel road that led to the trailer. She could take a boat on the river and RPG his ass. Not subtle, but definitely showy.

Hell, she could don hiking clothes, walk up to his door asking for help and put a .22 round through his eye.

And the ease of it was worrisome.

This kid was such a nobody. It wouldn't be much different than walking up to a random stranger and popping them. She was supposed to be impressing the Association, and she wasn't sure that wasting a twenty-something, trailer trash punk would even remotely accomplish that. She'd spent her career at the Association killing government officials, criminal bigwigs, whistleblowers and government agents. Hits against commoners were rarely something her organization indulged in unless someone wealthy felt they were a threat.

Well, her client hadn't considered the kid a threat at the time he'd contacted her, he just wanted revenge. And that client, though now deceased, had used the Association's services on more than one occasion in the past. Maybe that would be enough of a rationalization.

This couldn't just be about efficiency. It had to be performance art, a show for her employers, because she was already committed from the moment she'd sent in her initial report. She couldn't choose another assignment. The planning of the hit was more important than the culmination.

"Can't switch horses in mid-stream. I'll lose whatever minuscule amount of confidence the Association and the Council still have in me."

The bitch of it was, while she was good at killing, at getting in and out, she'd never had to plan an OP before. The Association had provided targets, supplied intel, as well as routes in and out. There'd always been a game plan and she'd followed the plans to the letter, only deviating when things went pear-shaped.

Like the Marine guard she'd had to knife at that embassy. He'd come upon her unexpectedly, and she'd stabbed him so hard she'd driven the blade into bone and couldn't get it out. She'd had to leave the knife behind. Not exactly subtle.

Or the OP that'd gotten her into this mess. Killing the wrong target, an ambassador's wife at that. That shitshow had surely required some innovative thinking to get clear.

On the other hand, she had a long history of successful OPs. The witness against a drug cartel. The politician in Venezuela who'd wanted a bigger cut of the local crime lord's business. The head of security who hadn't known when it was healthy to back off. And numerous others, all pulled off flawlessly.

Looking down at the little oasis that MacKenzie had carved out for himself, she thought, "Half this performance will need to be based on psych warfare. Maybe it's time to at least introduce myself."

And who knew? This might actually be fun.

9

"A toast, to a hell of an accomplishment." Uncle Gil said. "I can guarantee that no one else in our family history has ever run seventy-five miles before."

At Uncle Gil's toast, we all raised glasses of champagne and took a sip. It was one of the few times I'd ever tasted it, and I rather liked the bubbly concoction.

"That was a hell of a feat," Ed said, "Most I ever ran in one sitting was about twenty miles, and I was highly motivated by the Viet Cong being on our team's trail."

"I'd love to hear that story sometime," Vinnie said. "I've been in the position of doing a long-assed retreat, but never a run and gun. 'Specially not that far."

"It was not the best of times, Vinn. Lost half my team." Ed's eyes turned distant. Melinda looked at him with concern. Almost half a century after the end of the war, PTSD was still a real thing.

"So, Rosa, hear anything from your friend who got hurt during the race?" Mom was good at moving the topic away from sensitive subjects. Sometimes I wasn't sure that was a good thing.

"She texted me; sent a pic of herself in the hospital with a big dressing on her leg. She gave us a thumbs up," Rosa said.

"And once again apologized for getting hurt," I said. "Also for how her husband acted, like that was her fault somehow."

"Yeah. That was pretty f'd up," Rosa relied. "I had an officer in the sandbox who was like Dave. Nasty man. Really good at finding fault with everyone but himself. Didn't turn out well for him in the end."

Everyone was looking at her and the expectancy on our faces convinced her to explain. "See, our patrols in the town we were in kept telling him that the natives were getting restless. Pressure was building but the Captain said we were just being jumpy. Two days later our base was attacked, and he didn't keep his head down." Rosa mimed cocking a gun and shooting. "We had everyone defending the boundaries. Cooks, MPs like myself, and every Marine in the area. Fortunately, the second in command knew a few things and his strategies helped us hold the line until the cavalry came. Thank God." She crossed herself.

"That was a fricken mess over there," Vinnie said.

"Amen," Uncle Gil replied.

"So, do you two plan on running any more long races?" Melinda asked, trying to steer the subject away from war.

"Not with Dave!" Rosa and I said simultaneously.

"I'm not giving up the idea of marathons," Rosa explained. "But I think we're both done with team events. And, honestly, I don't really want to run any more than maybe a twenty-six miler. I can barely move today. I don't just ache in my tendons and muscles, I hurt in my joints. That can't be good for your body in the long run." She looked at me for confirmation.

"Yeah, same here. I like being in great shape, but I don't need to do something like that race to be in shape. I gotta wonder if some of those competitors are going to have to walk with canes and walkers when they retire."

"Probably wise," Uncle Gil said. "Now, if the team can move to my office, we have business to discuss."

"Oh *Madre de Dios*, Gilberto, it's almost three P.M. Surely we're not going to drive all the way to Oroville today."

"No, Rosa. We're not moving out today. Let's discuss it in my office where all the nice leather chairs and my whiteboard are."

———

The thickly padded leather chairs were a Godsend. Cool and smooth, so sensual. I could feel myself starting to nod off almost immediately.

"Nope. No. Rosa, Mac, you two take the oak chairs. You may not be able physically but I'm gonna need you to be fit mentally while I go over this. I need for you two to switch to the hard chairs." Uncle Gil told us. "Those over-stuffed chairs will put you two right to sleep."

Rosa and I didn't whine. No whining. But boy did we both groan as we had to stand up again. Astonishingly, neither Vinnie nor my uncle gave us a snide comment. Maybe they actually did respect what we'd accomplished.

Sitting on the hard seat didn't banish the tiredness. It was just uncomfortable enough that we weren't going to doze. When we'd gotten situated, Uncle Gil moved to his white-board "war map" and began pointing to blowups that he'd made on his expensive Epson printer.

"This is a blow-up of the Google Maps satellite photo of the vacation home of our quarry. As you can see, ex-county commissioner Richard 'Dick' Halstead must've had quite the building fund for the place."

"That," Vinnie said, a frown on his face, "looks like the

definition of a McMansion. How many rooms that place have?"

"According to the planning office, ten bedrooms, eight baths," Uncle Gil told us. "I was able to get a blueprint of the place from a local contact of mine. We know, as well as a ton of beds and baths, it also has three large open areas for 'entertaining' as well as several walk-in closets bigger than Mac's Airstream. Oh, and let's not forget the surround sound theater in the basement. And, I remind you, this is just his vacation home."

The amount of wealth that some people flaunted was almost inconceivable to anyone solidly middle-class. Unless we somehow came into a windfall of ridiculous proportions, no one in the room would ever own anything remotely this opulent.

"I sure wouldn't mind the money, but who needs a place like that?" I asked. "He have a big family or something? Or maybe he holds summits on world peace there?"

"He has a daughter, estranged, who has nothing to do with him. His ex-wife feels the same way. Evidently, when you shorten Richard's name, you're not just abbreviating, you're also describing the man's character." Uncle Gil told us. "As far as my contact could find out, the only one staying with him is his manservant, Eduardo Cerrano."

"Oh, I say!" Rosa said with an upper crust British accent that I bet would make most Brits roll their eyes if not cringe in pain. "Man servant! Mahn Suhrvant!"

"Maybe less a valet than someone to do dirty jobs that wouldn't pass the legality sniff test. Cerrano has a record, mostly low-level crimes, but he was almost convicted on an 'assault with a deadly weapon' charge. Less man servant, I think, than hired thug."

"Let me guess," Vinnie said. "He's not likely to take us

arresting his boss very well. Maybe he objects with strenuous violence."

"I sure wouldn't rule it out," Uncle Gil replied. "Lot of people don't really believe that bounty hunters count as agents of the court."

"So, when are you planning on going after this guy?" I asked.

"I'm going to give you and Rosa another day to heal up, then we're on. That McMansion is way too close to the Canadian border and our quarry could probably hoof it across anytime he wants. Hell, there are some old logging roads up there he could probably use to invade our neighbors to the north in a great big ol' SUV."

"How do we even know he's not across the border already?" Vinnie asked. "If I'd skipped bail on a corruption and embezzlement charge I sure wouldn't be hanging out where anyone who did some research could find me."

"The place is in his ex-wife's name," Uncle Gil said. "Evidently he's not supposed to have access any more. I'd guess that's why he's not had a visit from the local sheriff up there. But my contact in the area, who I'm paying a percentage to, has a very quiet drone he's flown over the place twice. He's seen our boy and Cerrano both times."

"Who's payin' us, Gil?" Vinnie asked. His long lanky 'surfer dude' self was sprawled on the leather couch, and Uncle Gil's cat, Mr. McGow, was curled up on his chest getting his ears scratched.

"Our local bail bonds sugar mama, Janna Morrison. And let me tell you, as a bail bonds person, Janna is sweating. Ex-commissioner Halstead had a sizable bail set by a local judge, a penalty for an indictment this severe, as well as a little bit of personal outrage penalty. Janna figured a county commissioner, even an ex-one, wouldn't be so crude as to skip bail." Uncle Gil gestured towards Halstead's photo on the board and shrugged. "Janna knew the guy, and I guess she figured he'd never want to let his reputation be 'sullied' by such behavior."

"She shoulda known, it's the 'respectable' ones that have the least honor," Rosa said. "How much is he into her for?"

Uncle Gil didn't answer immediately, and a slight upturn to the corners of his mouth made us all sit forward in our seats. Finally, he said, "Half million."

"Holy shit," Vinnie said. "No wonder she's sweating. Even if we get the dude back, our percentage is gonna hurt."

"I like Janna," Uncle Gil said, "but as much as I hate to admit it, I like her money even more." We all nodded, mercenary bastards that we were.

10

We'd planned on staying the night, but after a soak in the hot tub, both Rosa and I decided we wanted our own beds. I know that doesn't sound very romantic, but neither of us were going to feel 'romantic' for a day or two. It was a testament to how much we'd overtaxed our bodies. When you ache that much, you just want your own bed.

Back in Wenatchee, Rosa had leaned her head on my chest and sighed. "Sweetie, I'm sorry I'm not inviting you in, tonight, but…"

"I totally get it, babe," I said. "All I can think of is getting home, stretching a bit and going to sleep like the dead."

"You gonna be okay driving home? Honestly, I was so glad you drove us back here from Gil's. With your mom staying over there I…"

"You were able to sleep most of the way here," I said, chuckling. "I noticed, with no small amount of jealousy, I might add. But nah, I can make it home okay. I'm tired, but not falling asleep at the wheel tired."

"*Bueno.*" She kissed me lightly and trudged up the stairwell to her second story apartment, giving me a little wave as she went. I turned back to the parking lot to retrieve my dusty rusty pickup, the Doom Mobile.

It was just before sunset, the 'hour of long shadows' as my friend and mentor Jim Threefeathers calls it. Purplish shadows from the surrounding buildings and the trees that the developers had managed to save criss-crossed the pavement as I turned the key in my door lock.

Then one of the shadows moved.

The end of the new shadow stopped six inches from my toe and resolved into a head with two large upright canine-looking ears. I looked up to where it had to be coming from, and of course, there was nothing there. Looking down to my foot, the shadow had vanished too.

There's only one entity it could have been. The Trickster that had shown up in my life numerous times to warn me that death was near and hunting me. Jim Threefeathers said it was *Sen K'lip*, the Coyote God. The Yakama nation to the south of me called him *Spilyay*. Every native American tribe had a name for the Trickster.

And for some reason, The King, as I called him, had taken a liking to me. I have no idea why. But when he began randomly showing up, it was his way of saying, "Keep your head on a swivel, Boy. Something' ain't right."

I got in my pickup and after a few shuddering cranks, it turned over and I started back toward the Malaga Highway, my head on a swivel.

———

It takes a while to get through Wenatchee. To more urban-dwelling people our city might seem small, but we've been blessed with an inordinate number of bad drivers, much higher I'm sure than the national average.

I'd unwisely decided to take Wenatchee Avenue through

town, which turned into the Malaga Highway outside of the city limits. Seemed like a reasonable idea, but part way through the main business area, I was stuck mid-block by an impressive fender bender between two people who had no clue about getting their still functional cars off the street. Instead, they blocked the two-lane section of the avenue and yelled at each other.

I was stopped, unable to move forward, unable to back up. Someone a couple cars ahead walked up to them, I assumed to ask them to pull over into one of the parking lots on the street below. The good Samaritan finally wound up walking away as the two offenders yelled at his back. No good deed goes unpunished.

Someone must've called the authorities, because the cops showed up. By the time they got there and in no uncertain terms told the idiots to move their cars, we'd been sitting stationary a good half hour. The sun was gone, and a deep twilight was on the land. By the time I left the edge of town, it was close to dark.

Twilight is a worrisome time to drive in our area. We have a healthy deer population, along with jack rabbits, raccoons and even the cousins of the one who'd contacted me in the parking lot. Collecting their corpses was a full-time job for a select group working for the Washington Department of Transportation. The corpses often wound up with our local wildlife rehabilitators as food for the animals who'd survived.

The trick to successful navigation at this time of day/night is to have one eye on the side of the road. Usually, if you're watching carefully, you can see the reflection of eyes looking toward the bright lights of your vehicle. If you see even the hint of such a reflection, slow down right then. Otherwise, it's a bloodied dent in your car along with a guilty conscience. Or worse.

By the time I'd reached brightly-lit Rock Island Dam, I'd

managed to avoid two deer, a raccoon and a stray cat, all probably heading down to the Columbia River for a drink.

I was two miles past the dam, driving in full dark, when Death side-swiped me.

One moment I was driving along, wanting nothing more than to be home. The next, a black pickup (or maybe it was an SUV) was rushing at me, across the line in my lane. No lights. Moving very fast. Coming head on.

If I hadn't been half-exhausted, I might've made it past unscathed, but I took an extra half-second to get the wheel cranked over and the fast-moving maniac's vehicle side-swiped me, scraping the side of the Doom Mobile and taking off my driver's side mirror.

"Shit!" I yelled, as the right front wheel of my pickup caught in the soft sand of the shoulder. The sand yanked my steering wheel sideways and the Doom Mobile tipped over on its side and plowed dirt for twenty feet, stopping in a stand of thick sagebrush.

Dust settling all around me, I hung in place, trying to get my heart to stop attempting to beat its way out of my chest. Somehow, the dash lights were still on, giving me a tiny amount of visibility. I struggled to get out of my seatbelt without falling onto the passenger side door. Hanging on to the strap, I was able to swing my feet in that direction, but when I tried to unlock the seatbelt I was hanging from, the latch wouldn't open.

My pocket knife wasn't clipped where it should be, the thigh pocket of my cargo pants. Looking down, I saw a glint against the doorframe below me I was pretty sure was the knife.

"Nice work, pocket clip. You had one flippin' job." I said, bringing my left foot as high as I could. Reaching into my sock, I extracted the tiny serrated-edge Spyderco knife I kept there as a backup and began sawing. A moment later I dropped feet-first onto the passenger side door.

Extracting my keys from the ignition, I turned on the tiny LED flashlight attached to it and surveyed my situation. I might make it out of the driver-side door if I wanted to climb. I braced my feet on the open glove compartment and pulled the door latch. It was going to be a pain to open the door upward like a submarine hatch, but I found the point was moot.

The door wasn't budging. Probably damaged by the other truck. And with the truck lying on its side, I obviously wasn't going out the passenger door. Looking around with the light, I saw the windshield was cracked and crackled all the way across. Tucking my hand down into my Carhartt jacket sleeve, and gripping the cutaway seatbelt buckle, I smashed it out the rest of the way. I squirmed out through the broken glass, dust and sagebrush. Getting to my feet, I began shaking uncontrollably.

It had nothing to do with the temperature.

———

It took me nearly two hours to finally make it home.

After talking to the Chelan County Sheriff's deputy and letting EMTs treat various small cuts and abrasions, all the while doing my best to convince them I didn't need to go to the hospital, the deputy at the scene dropped me off at the end of the pavement near my home. I promised to stop by CCS headquarters in the morning to file a formal report, though I didn't know what I could add to what I'd already told him.

I was carrying my get home bag and my small tool bag, having retrieved them from the Doom Mobile before it was towed. I didn't bother to take the old blankets and left the passenger door unlocked. If one of Wenatchee's growing number of homeless people wanted them, they wouldn't have to break a side window to get them.

I had no idea if the truck was safe to drive, but my favorite mechanic could tell me after she found the old girl in her parking lot in the morning. I still would need a ride into town tomorrow, but I was pretty sure that Rosa would come through for me there.

"10:35 p.m. No reason to freak out my friends and loved ones until the morning," I said to myself as I put the phone back in my pocket. I walked past my mom's dark ranch house and down the dirt track that led to my property.

There is very little light pollution out my way. You can see a slight glow from Wenatchee to the west, but it's very faint. To the east, there was an even fainter glow from the farming community of Quincy, but your eyes would need to be at full dilation to notice either of them in the night sky.

What really stood out was the universe. The sky was perfectly clear, and with my night vision maxed out I instantly picked out my old friend Polaris, the North Star. Not as bright as you'd expect such a useful point of light to be, but its position between The Big Dipper and Cassiopeia was ever unchanging over the northern axis of the Earth. These were the first stars I'd memorized when I was a teen-aged student at the Seeker School, the wilderness training campus where I'd learned the basics of my nature skills.

The landscape around me was black, but the lighter strip of the dirt road was easy to follow. I stepped carefully, lightly touching down with the ball of my foot before committing my weight. I had a second small tactical flashlight in my pocket, extracted from the get home bag, but using it would mean I'd lose all my night vision. Having just avoided death earlier, I was loath to give up this magical experience just to have a little light I could do without anyway.

That changed when I made it to the switch-backed driveway down to my home. The road down was formed from crushed brown basalt (and not crushed that fine) and was almost indistinguishable from the surrounding landscape in the darkness. I had no desire to wander off the steep embankments supporting it. The flashlight got me to my trailer.

It was when I stepped onto my deck/porch and the motion light activated that I saw the piece of paper stuck to my door.

"Who'd be leaving me notes way out here?" I hoped it wasn't one of the occasional self-righteous hikers who felt there should be no private ownership of land out here next to the wildlife refuge. About once a year, I had to threaten calling the cops to get some overbearing clodhopper out of my face when I was on my own porch. It was one reason, remote as I was, that I always locked my door whenever I left home.

I pulled the note, more of a folded card, off the door. Unfolding it and turning so that the light from the motion lamp was on it, I saw a drawing printed in black ink. It was very well-done, but its artistic merit was lost in the message it conveyed: it was a very stylized picture of the grim reaper surrounded by a wreath of roses. If I'd seen it in a gift shop, I'd have thought *cool drawing*. Stuck to my door it wasn't cool at all, it was threatening.

The brief handwritten message below the art didn't make things better. It simply read: *See you soon.*

11

"Christ, that was good." She said to herself. "I'm all tingly."

After leaving her calling card, she'd waited on her prey's porch, and monitored his progress through her very illegal version of the Find my Phone app. With that, she'd been able to watch his progress back to his trailer and knew just when to meet him on the road.

Waiting along the deserted highway, sitting in the all-black stolen truck until young MacKenzie had passed the dam, she'd gone to meet him. And damn, it'd be a long time before he forgot that meeting.

"I bet he pissed himself!" The very idea made her even more tingly, the thought that she'd inspired so much terror in her mark that he'd have lost bladder control. "Hoo! Rein it in, Marjie. This is a professional job, not a game. Rein it in. Chill."

As she'd hurtled toward MacKenzie's twin headlights though, she'd almost lost it. For a moment, she'd almost not swerved. Somehow the thought of going to whatever was... after... together with her prey had almost taken over.

She didn't believe in an afterlife. No rewards, no judgments, but sometimes she wondered if she was wrong. Sometimes, she almost wanted to find out for sure. No more stress of being alive, not for her or for young MacKenzie. Who knew? Maybe taking his life would be doing him a favor.

But she couldn't let her crazier impulses run the show. She was a professional with a job to do. She still had a lot of good years, prime years. She could find out what happened post-death when she was old, ugly and falling apart.

Sadly for MacKenzie, he wasn't going to have that option.

12

The next morning I awoke sore in even more new places thanks to the crash. I was beginning to think 'achey all over' was my new normal.

I called Rosa, and told her what had happened on my way home, and to beg a ride in to Wenatchee. There wasn't exactly a lot of bus service out this far. It took me long enough to calm her down that I decided to delay telling the rest of my family. My mom, even though she was an ER nurse, would still likely be hysterical, while Uncle Gil might well find some way in which the whole thing was my fault.

I sat there in my deck chair waiting and meditating on what had happened. I might've shrugged the calling card off as someone screwing with me, but combined with the near fatal, almost-head-on crash, I admitted to myself I was spooked. The whole thing was creepy as hell.

"Maybe it *is* the grim reaper taking physical form?"

I let my mind freewheel with that goofy idea for a while, actually inadvertently writing the story in my head before rejoining the real world. Eventually I dredged up some mental discipline from somewhere and engaged in some actual analytical thought.

"Someone decided to play chicken last night. Is it connected to the card?" I asked the great blue heron wading along the shore. "Was the driver just a drunk, driving down the road with no headlights in a black-as-night truck?"

The heron didn't seem too responsive to this train of thought.

"Or is someone actually out to get me?" I jumped slightly as the heron, a good fifty yards away let out a raucous "GRONK" and flew off down river. If I was a person who actually believed in portents and signs I would've been even more spooked.

Then I remembered the shadow in Rosa's parking lot, and a chill went down my spine.

———

"Sure sounds like a threat to me," Rosa said. "Back in the Barrio in LA, if Id'a received a note like that, I would have been looking for a way to get a gun, and I would've carried it in my bag everywhere." She looked over at me from the RAV's driver seat. "I don't know if I ever told you this, Mac, but I went into the Marines as a way to avoid getting involved in a gang war. The less said about that, though, the better."

"Damn, Rosa. That sounds intense. Leaving an LA war to fight in a foreign war."

"Believe me, it was the safer choice, for me and my family. But back to this card, I find it hard to believe that the card and the death pickup aren't somehow related."

"I've come to the same conclusion. My reaction time was poor last night, and I'm pretty sure that the black pickup swerved at the last second. I'm also pretty sure they were intending to just run me off the road. My reflexes are damn good, and normally I'd have dodged them."

"So you think someone's trying to put a scare into you?"

"Maybe? If so, they succeeded. Though I'm having a hard time coming up with anyone who'd hate me that much. All my real enemies, the one's I'd consider first, are either in prison or dead. There may be some small fry that we've returned to custody, but if it's one of them, why target just me?

"Are you sure it's just you?" she replied. "Maybe the whole team needs to be cautious."

"Too early to tell. My gut tells me this is something different from just playing shitty pranks, though."

"America's changed a lot over the last few years," Rosa said. "A lot more free-roaming crazy out there."

———

In Wenatchee, we stopped at the Chelan County Sheriff's headquarters for me to file a formal report regarding the accident. As it happened, my buddy deputy sheriff Dave Mathews was in the office; I showed him the card and told him our suppositions. Most officers would've probably just told me to file another report, but Dave knew my history.

"What is it with you, Mac?" He asked. "I swear, trouble is drawn to you like iron shavings to a magnet."

"Thank you!" Rosa said. "I've been telling him he's a trouble magnet for years, Dave,"

"Remember what Obi Wan said about fools following," I told her. She punched me in the arm. "I mean, I must also be a magnet for gorgeous, strong women too, right?"

"Good save, Mac," Dave said. "But all I can do at the moment is write a report, and note your ability to find deadly opponents. We don't even remotely have the manpower to put someone on stakeout at your place. The sheriff would laugh me out of the office."

"I feel safer already," I deadpanned.

"Sorry man, I wish..."

"I didn't expect that there was much the sheriff's department could do besides look for a scuffed up black pickup or SUV, license unknown, with my side mirror embedded in its hood. Really, I just want this noted, in case something more tangible happens to me."

"Consider it noted." Dave said.

Rosa drove me to Dina Torelli's garage on South Wenatchee Avenue to see if the Doom Mobile was salvageable. We had to park a ways down the street because some of her mechanical clients were parked on the Ave, so that the large number of cars to be worked on could be juggled with those waiting.

"I don't see the DM," Rosa said. "Maybe Dina took one look and decided to sell it for scrap."

"If so, she probably would've done it before I even had the accident. My poor old girl was no beauty to begin with."

In the office, Dina was behind the counter talking to José, her lead mechanic. José went back into the work area, and Dina waved us over. Dina was in her mid-forties and had started out as gopher for her former employer, Ned Pearson. She learned to be a damn fine mechanic with Ned's tutelage, but she'd proven to be an even better business woman. She eventually bought out her mentor, whose drinking problem was threatening to sink the whole thing, then employed him part-time as a mechanic. In the end, she'd even helped him quit the booze.

A few years ago, Rosa and I had gotten private investigator licenses to supplement our bounty hunting credentials/skills. Dina had come to us because her ex-husband was demanding visitation rights for the first time in her ten-year-old son's life. Dina had heard things about her ex's lifestyle and wanted us to check him out before she would even consider the idea of his having access to the boy.

It was a good thing she'd done so. Her ex-husband had turned from a semi-respectable working man into a fentanyl addict whose lucid moments didn't really improve his judgment or sense of responsibility.

She took the proof we provided to court, telling the judge (through her lawyer) that she could live with her ex never paying child support, but she sure didn't want her son exposed to the tender ministrations of an addict. Needless to say, she won easily. She even got a restraining order.

"So, I bet you're here to check up on that death trap I found parked near my car enclosure this morning, eh, Mac?"

"Hey Dina," I said. "Yeah. Someone ran me off the road on the way home last night. Have you had a chance to take a look at her? Is the old gal salvageable?"

"With a name like the Doom Mobile, who knows? But we're kinda swamped. I always try to give you and Rosa a little extra service, but I have to be fair to the other customers. Ned's in tomorrow, and I'll have him give your "classic" pickup the once over. If it's still drivable, I'll let you know, but if the frame's too bent, you'll definitely have to let it go. As for the body work, well, let's be honest, the new dents and dings hardly make a difference in your truck's beauty."

"Ouch."

"Sorry, Mac. I know the truth hurts."

"I didn't buy her to impress anyone," I said. "Just basic transportation to all the wild places I wind up going."

"Actually, he bought her because she was cheap," Rosa said, speaking out the side of her mouth. "Just sayin..."

"Oh, Rosa," Dina shook her head, "have you hitched your wagon to a cheapskate?"

"Okay, okay," I said. "There's nothing wrong with being frugal. Can I go get a few things out of the Doom Mobile's cab?"

Dina gave Rosa an exaggerated wink, an exercise that definitely needed a lot more practice, and directed me toward the back door. That exit came out in the chain link security fence enclosure that she kept client's cars in.

She ran an equal opportunity garage. There were BMW's, KIA's Honda's and even an old VW bus that someone was making into a motorhome. Plenty of shiny cars and trucks. Then, at the end of the lot, the dilapidated beastie I'd been driving the last few years. Most of the time I didn't think about how ugly she was, but placed in a lot full of nice-looking cars, it almost seemed she was self-conscious.

"I kinda got used to how beat up she is, Mac," Rosa said. "But I think we have to admit your truck is the most God-awful looking thing in here."

"Shhhh, Rosa! She'll hear you." I patted the rust-spotted hood. "There, there, baby. Rosa didn't mean it. You're my good girl. We'll get you going again if it's at all possible. Don't you worry."

Rosa rolled her eyes and tried to open the dented driver-side door. It wouldn't budge. She walked around me as I continued to calm the worries of my faithful steed and opened the passenger door. I noticed when she looked in and stiffened.

"What is it, Rosa?"

"I see your knife on the floor, Mac," she said, looking around the perimeter of the fence. "But it seems there's something else here."

The concern in her voice made me come over to her and

take a look for myself. Lying on the seat was another folded card. I didn't want to pick it up, but I had to.

Unfolded, it had the same lush Grim Reaper artwork and another hand-written annotation underneath. *"Quite the thrill, wasn't it, MacKenzie? Don't worry, it'll all be over soon."*

13

While it wasn't much as campaigns went, she had to admit that she was starting to enjoy the game.

She'd gotten the calling card idea from a movie she'd watched about assassins, and damn did Hollywood get the details ninety percent wrong. But there'd been one thing that Marjory had taken away from the flick: having a sense of style. That was when she'd started leaving the cards where they could eventually be found.

She didn't write anything on them in her professional hits, and only left them on those jobs that someone wanted it known they weren't accidents. Usually these were criminal on criminal jobs. On a few such obvious hits, she'd left the cards just for the sheer brass of it. And to let everyone know that the deceased had pissed off someone enough that they'd hired a professional.

This was something the Association hadn't needed to know about. They understood efficiency, but not style. Leaving the cards was almost like an artist signing their work.

She'd never considered actually signing them or much less writing a note, but this job was different. Psych warfare required sending your target a clear message (because you never knew how dense people could be these days) and that's what she'd done to young Crow.

It bothered her slightly, aiming her skills at a twenty-something, clueless, small town hick. Her irritation wasn't for any moral reason. It was because she had the nagging feeling that such an easy kill wouldn't impress the people she needed desperately to impress.

Well, she'd smother those people with style. The target didn't matter, doing it with style and efficiency was what counted.

She still couldn't go all the way with the kid just yet, but she had an escalating plan for foreplay. It would suck to be MacKenzie Crow, but that was life.

And death.

14

"So you've gotten two notes now?"

"Yeah, Uncle Gil. The first one punctuated with me being run off the road."

Rosa had convinced me that it was time to let our group know what was happening. My mom, still staying at Uncle Gil's farm, went right into semi-hysterical worrying parent mode.

Rosa and I sent a photo of the second note to Dave at the sheriff's department, but we'd brought the second physical card for Uncle Gil to look at. Vinnie also stayed the night and was currently giving the note a careful examination.

"Man, Gil," he said. "I don't know any other way to take this. Note's definitely a threat."

"Or a warning," Melinda said, sitting next to my mom and patting her on the shoulder.

"I'd go with threat," Ed told her. "When I was in the Nam, some of our Spec Ops group, when we ambushed an NVA patrol, would leave playing cards lying on the bodies. One guy had a deck special printed that was all Ace of

Spades, and let me tell you, it spooked Charlie bad. This has that vibe."

"Trying to spook us," Rosa said. "They're doing a good job of it. When we were driving out here, I was watching every car that got near us. Drive-bys might not be a thing here in North Central Washington, but I still have no desire to be a part of one."

"Gil, you need to do something to keep my kids safe," Mom said. "I knew that his going into the bounty hunting business with you would somehow get him killed, someday. And sure enough, here we are."

"Um.. Mom? You know I'm sitting right here, and I'm not dead, right?"

"You know what I mean, Mac. Gil? What are we going to do?"

"Mac made the choice to continue on in our field, Sis. After what happened in Kauai, we had a long talk about it, and he said he found purpose in bringing scumbags back to justice. He also informed me, in no uncertain terms, that he was a grown-up and outside of business, all I was allowed to do was advise. Rosa seconded that, by the way."

I felt Rosa's hand creep into mine as she spoke, "We also don't know if this has anything to do with the bounty hunting business. I'll remind everyone that almost every time Mac and I have had trouble, it was during outside activities. Kauai was the only exception that I can think of."

"No matter where it's coming from," Uncle Gil said, "there's definitely danger here." He looked out the living room window. Rosa and I didn't mention the huge coyote we knew so well had stepped out of the sagebrush and plunked himself right in our path as we'd been driving down the driveway. The King had simply looked at us. Intently. None of the tongue-lolling humor we saw emanating from him on most of his sightings. Just a deadly intense gaze directed at us and a clear message.

This shit's real.

Then, as usual, he disappeared into the sagebrush sea. Rosa saw him as well as I did, which seemed to happen when we were *both* in danger.

"Someone is handling this like a pro, or at least a semi-pro," Uncle Gil told us. "I need to make a few calls, see if I can get any intel. Until further notice, Mac and Rosa, I want you to stay out here."

I started to reflexively protest, being a bit riled up from my mother trying to run my life, but Rosa laid a palm on my forearm. "I think that would be a wise plan, Gilberto. It's not like we have pets we need to take care of. But... are we not going after the corrupt commissioner?"

"I think we can still do that. We'll be quite a ways away from home, and no one knows where we're going outside of the team. Vinnie and I can stop by the office and get all the gear late tonight. We can leave early the following day."

"Or we can just pick it up on the way out of town," Vinnie said. "I assume we're gonna be leaving well before first light. I mean, let's save a trip."

Uncle Gil seemed satisfied with that, and we all felt a bit better at just getting out of town for a while. Almost all of us.

Mom did not look happy, not in the least, and I couldn't really blame her.

15

We spent one day at the farm, then we were on our way north.

I was happy to get going. As crazy as it sounds for someone who lives as remotely as I do, staying at my uncle's farm always makes me feel antsy. I'm pretty sure it has to do with being under Uncle Gil's scrutiny, not the remoteness. I may be a grown-ass man, but the feeling that I'm not quite living up to his "John Wayne-ish" ideals never seems to go away.

A part of me knows I'm being ungrateful. Uncle Gil was the primary male role model I've had since my father died when I was a very small boy. He is Gen-X old school and doesn't tolerate either weakness or foolishness. This has led to us butting heads on numerous occasions, as I am not exactly a wallflower myself.

Or, as Rosa sums it up more succinctly: "Men!"

The four of us, Gil, Vinnie, Rosa and I, had left the farm at 4:00 a.m., stopped at the office to pick up the "action bags" that Vinnie had pre-packed so that they were always ready, and got on the road for Okanogan County.

I was driving, and Uncle Gil raised an eyebrow when I crossed the Columbia River to drive the highway that paralleled the eastern shore.

"97?" he asked, referring to the highway we were emerging onto. "Don't like 97-A in the dark?" 97-A was the roadway that went up the western side of the river and gradually emerged into, and passed through, the city of Chelan. It was a picturesque drive at the base of tall cliffs and mountains, its track practically being right next to the mighty Columbia.

"We'll bypass Chelan this way, Uncle Gil. Also, as dark as it still is, I'd like to not have an unscheduled impact with a desert bighorn on the way. This is the time of day they tend to get on the roadway on their way back from the river to the hillsides."

"Good call all around," he replied, "but going this way there's a lot of orchards, so you have the deer in the headlights problem."

"I'll be careful. If you want to take a nap like Rosa and Vinnie are, this is the time."

He chuckled. "All right, I can take a hint." He tilted his seat back slightly and closed his eyes. After about a minute, his breathing deepened into the slow in-and-out draws of sleep.

Around ten miles down the road, I had a near-miss encounter with a skunk, only seeing the flash of red in its eyes at the last second. Fortunately, a quick swerve avoided the little stink-bomb by inches. I breathed a prayer of thanks. If Uncle Gil and the others had woken up to a war-wagon reeking of dead skunk, I'd have never heard the end of it.

Looking in the mirror, I saw that my car-o-batics hadn't woken any of my sleeping companions. I settled in with my thoughts for the long drive ahead. Driving a car in the dark, you have a lot of opportunity to think about things. And of course, those thoughts went instantly to the card-leaving, chicken-playing asshole who was making my life... interesting.

Uncle Gil mentioned my assailant seeming like a semi-pro, but I didn't see it. Leaving a note on my door while I was away? Not much skill required there. Picking the lock on Dina's car enclosure? Okay, a bit more skill, but anyone on our team could've picked that Master Lock in about twenty seconds with the right tools.

But... the meeting me on the Malaga Highway... All indications were that they'd gone to my house, left the note, and somehow knew I was on my way back, something I hadn't even known until Rosa and I decided not to stay out at the farm.

Which could mean only one thing. It meant that whoever it was... had the ability to track me.

Crap!

Maybe there was a tracker on the Doom Mobile which allowed that black truck to meet me on the highway.

After thinking about it, I was sure the driver had swerved at the last second, my own reflexes being impaired by my fatigue. Then, they'd known right where my bashed-up truck had been taken. All it would take would be an air-tag surreptitiously placed in the truck while it was in Rosa's parking lot.

But there was another way, assuming that they had good, but illegal, tech support. They could've tracked me with my iPhone. Law enforcement does this all the time, though civilians aren't supposed to be able to do so unless the person being tracked is part of their own cellular plan.

The Find-My-Phone app allowed me to know where any one of our group's phones were thanks to satellite technology and the hardware in the phone that allowed location tracking. We were all on the same Verizon plan, paid for by our business. It was tax deductible that way.

If my suspicions were correct, assuming you could track one of us, theoretically you could track all of us.

When my friend Kailee was pursued by a powerful man a few years ago and came to us for help, Uncle Gil immediately got rid of her phone. He'd put it in the baggage compartment of an east-bound Greyhound bus, never to be seen (or tracked) again. It threw the enemy off for a little while.

If your opponent has the right tech, your personal phone can be a serious liability.

———

Uncle Gil opened his eyes an hour later and looked out at the orange sky heralding eminent sunrise. When his grogginess passed, I told him my thoughts on the matter.

"If this is true," he said, "if they're able to track your phone, then this person definitely might well have some connections with either organized crime or some sort of government three-letter agency."

"I'm still stumped on why I'm in the crosshairs."

"At this point, Mac, the why is the last thing to worry about. *Who, where,* and *what* are the priorities, in that order. If we learn who's involved, the why might take care of itself. Either way, your idea makes enough sense that I don't really feel like we can take a chance with our phones."

"We've all got them with us," I said. "If we're being phone tracked, then they know we're heading north. All of us."

"But that's all they know. Mac, take the next turn-off, the one that goes toward Electric City."

"That's a bit out of the way, Gil," Vinnie said, showing he'd not only been awake, but listening. "What's your plan?"

"Two-fold. One, it's going away from the destination we're actually going to, laying a false trail. There's also a post-office there. We'll package up Mac and Rosa's phones and send them Priority-mail to our office. In fact, since we're all on the same phone plan, Vinn, you and I better add our phones to the package as well."

I turned the War Wagon onto a side road leading toward Grand Coulee Dam, and its attendant township, Electric City. Rosa quietly asked: "We gonna get burner phones, Gil? Maybe at the Walmart in Omak?"

"Good God," he said, laughing, "you two can go without phones for a day or two. We've got the radios for our OP against the commissioner. Do you good to unplug for a while." Rosa gave him a flat look in return.

"Honestly, I'm perfectly happy to be unreachable for a few days after all that's happened." I said. Rosa turned her flat stare to me as I continued. "But while you're packaging up our phones, I think I'm gonna go over the vehicle with a sharp eye, looking for electronic trackers."

"All three of us will," Vinnie said. "I don't know how anyone could've gotten access to the gear in our office, but from what Mac said about the locks at Dina's bein' picked, nothing's out of the question. I'm gonna pull everything out of those bags and make sure no one's stuck an AirTag or two in 'em. I mean, you can literally buy tracking tags on Amazon."

"I'll take the engine section," Rosa said. "I helped my Uncle down in L.A. in his shop enough, I'm pretty sure I can spot anything out of place in that area."

"Good. Good initiative, all of you," Gil said, without looking back, "It's better to be safe than sorry. To paraphrase the old quote: just because you're paranoid doesn't mean they're not out to track you."

16

Marjory was up bright and early, sipping a gingerbread latte and eating a scone in a much nicer coffee shop than the City of Wenatchee deserved. She'd picked up her consumables from the counter and found a booth in the corner so she could watch the room. No one could see what she was looking at on the iPad.

It was a stunningly beautiful fall morning, leaves just starting to turn, sky a deep clear cloudless blue, temperature absolutely perfect. A part of her had yearned to grab one of the outdoor tables on the side-walk, but when you lived a life like hers, paranoid caution was deeply ingrained. It was almost a form of hyper-vigilance. Sort of a PTSD. Outdoor booths wouldn't be safe.

The app she was using, supplied by the Association's tame tech gurus, could be monitored from anywhere she had cell service or WIFI. And any shithead who tried to access her device through the open networks like the coffee shops was in for a rude surprise. Another App, supplied by her associate DevilKnight243, would spike the hell out of anyone's unauthorized device trying to access her own.

Yesterday Marjory had watched young MacKenzie Crow weave his way around this backwater, hitting the sheriff's office, and then the mechanic's yard.

A smile came over her face as she imagined him seeing the second card. She'd counted coup on him once again. She'd have to ramp things up next time. Ratchet up the stress and document the effects.

His signal had gone out to the farm his uncle owned and hadn't moved. She switched through monitoring the phones of all his close associates and was surprised to note that all four signals were coming from the same place.

"Y'all having a sleepover, then?" She'd laughed at the thought and gone to bed.

But now, a day later, it looked like all four of them were out of the area, which was unexpected. Maybe out on a bounty hunting expedition? The Canadian border was up that way. Had she spooked Crow enough that he was aiming to cross it? It wouldn't save him, but it would be a pain in the ass. She'd done her planning around the prey's home area.

Marjory didn't like the unexpected. It made her feel out of control, and, above all things, she didn't like being out of control.

The phones were in movement, then had gone stationary.

She'd watched them stay in the same place for several hours and her intuition was telling her that something was wrong.

She clicked on the icon for MacKenzie's iPhone, and her app interfaced with Google Maps. Running her stylus over the same spot in Google, a small popup with an arrow appeared. The popup read: Electric City Post office.

"Dammit! The kid's smarter than he looks."

She unfolded the Washington State map she'd bought and grimaced at all the back ways, farm roads and even dirt roads that showed up. Even as low as the population was in the area, that was a lot of territory.

"This kid's dossier reputes him to be a master outdoorsman. He gets into Canada, he could vanish into the Coastal range, and I'd never find him in time to save my ass. From everything I learned about him, the little fucker could put a pack on his back and disappear out there indefinitely."

Marjory almost never panicked, but this mission was becoming much more difficult than she had anticipated. She thought she had time to play with her prey. A normal mission, you went in, hit the target quickly and efficiently, and you got your ass out. But this cluster fuck of her own making required too much time.

Too much time for the mark to figure out what was going on.

Her heart rate sped up, and she felt short of breath. It took all of the meditation techniques Timothy had shown her to get her equilibrium back. She began to crave her little secret back in her room.

She couldn't do this without help. And there was only one person who could, and still would help her.

DevilKnight243.

17

It was a gorgeous day to be outside, even if it was to take a fugitive into custody. Sun rays slanted through the tall pines in columns of light usually reserved for religious paintings. Stellars jays called from the treetops, and as I sat crouched behind some low-lying scrub brush, I saw a deer and her half-grown fawn walk past the house we were watching.

The Okanogan country was a pretty area. Different than the areas closer to the Cascades, less dense in its pine forests, making for farther-viewed vistas. Once we'd left the dam, we'd gone north along a backroad eventually leading us to our destination, though in a roundabout way.

The landscape had turned from dry grass/sagebrush land and wheat fields to the beginnings of forests and finally, rich, uncluttered pine canopy. Soon, the only ugly spots were the occasional remains of forest fires.

If I myself owned the home ex-commissioner Halstead was currently occupying (or at least we hoped he was), I would've moved the trees back from the house a good hundred yards in every direction. I wouldn't have liked destroying the gorgeous shade-providing pines, but all it would take would be one nasty forest fire coming through, and only a superhuman effort would keep the buildings from becoming charcoal.

Rather than walking right up to the door, Uncle Gil decided it would be best if we went covert and surveilled the house for a while to see if we could make visual contact with our prey. Knowing for certain the fugitive was on the premises would greatly enhance our legal options.

Bounty hunters can enter the home of a fugitive or access their property, especially if they know the person is on the premises. No warrant needed. The minor sticking point here was that the house was in Halstead's ex-wife's name, but we all doubted she'd object. Her ex-husband wasn't even supposed to have access to the place.

Stakeouts can be interminable, seeming to last forever, especially if you're waiting for someone to come home. I doubted Dick Halstead was likely to have gone anywhere, there being a warrant for his arrest, and his face on every Washington State news source. Ex-commissioner turned fugitive was kinda big news in our neck of the woods. I hoped that we'd get this show on the road soon, since we were *pretty* sure he was in there, thanks to Uncle Gil's contact in the area.

We were stationed at the four corners of the place, several hundred yards out, watching with binoculars. All we needed was for our man to step outside for a smoke or maybe just a breath of fresh air. So far, we hadn't seen any sign of Halstead or his lackey Cerrano, but a large black SUV sat in the dust-covered asphalt driveway. I could tell from the way the dust was shifted around that it had been driven in and out all week. The plates weren't any that were registered to the ex-commissioner, but what fugitive drives around in their own, undoubtedly searched for, vehicle?

Normally Rosa and I, being at different points of the compass, would be texting while we waited, assuming there was cell signal. Now, of course, we had no phones and were all left alone with our thoughts, our only means of communication being the small radios on our belts. Uncle Gil had told us to use them as little as possible, though. A smart fugitive would have a scanner to listen to the local radio chatter, and some of those could switch frequencies when a nearby signal was detected.

I was quite surprised when a dusty pickup with an equally dusty canopy showed up. Uncle Gil and I were watching the front, and I could just see him at his southwest observation point. He looked at me and gave an exaggerated shrug, holding his hands palms upward as if to say, "What the hell?"

We got our answers a moment later as Eduardo Cerrano climbed out of the driver-side door, moving around to the back hatch of the canopy. Through my binoculars, I watched him pull out boxes of what looked like supplies and set them on the now lowered tailgate. As he carried a box inside, I heard dry pine needles crunching coming from my left. Looking that way, I saw Uncle Gil approaching.

"Mac," he said, " see if you can make out what's in that remaining box on the tailgate."

"Will do. I can also see there's more stuff farther back from the tailgate that Cerrano hasn't pulled out yet."

"Maybe they're planning on forting up. What do you see in that box on the tailgate?"

"This is kinda weird, Uncle Gil. It's not groceries, or at least not groceries for the house. I'm seeing... backpacking food! Packages of the freeze-dried stuff and a butane cartridge, one of the small ones for a backpacking stove."

"Move around a bit so that you can see in the back of the truck. I'm thinking our boys might be planning a little cross-country trip to Canada."

I did as I was bid. Moving around counter clockwise, I reached a bushy area where I could see in the back. A pair of dark green Osprey backpacks were sitting on their sides on the truck bed. Through the binoculars, I could still see the sales tags hanging from them. I reported this to Uncle Gil.

"Team, get ready to move up," he said through his radio. "Looks like our mark is planning on hoofing it northward. Mac, how far away did you say the border is?"

"Just under ten miles," I replied, "most people could do it in a day if they had to, depending on their physical condition."

"Move in close to the house," he said to the radio again. "Let's risk sneaking a look in the windows. All we need now is to make visual contact with Halstead and we can go in."

We moved up across the cursedly-crunchy pine needles and hid behind the truck. I peeked around the right rear corner of the dusty pickup. "Uncle Gil, I think we can cat-foot right up to the house and start sneaking peeks."

He nodded and we moved up, staying low as we went. Uncle Gil split off toward the western edge of the house, while I went onto the porch to see if I could catch a glimpse through the big picture window in the front.

Neither of us was quite in position when the gunshot rang out.

18

I don't care how much of a cool cucumber you are, when a shot rings out near you, you are at the very least going to flinch, and most likely duck your head. I had barely recovered my equilibrium and headed up the front steps, Uncle Gil not far behind, when the front door slammed open.

Eduardo Cerrano came barreling out the door like a freight train. I barely had time to note the large duffle slung over one shoulder before he hit me with all the force of a pro football player, knocking the wind out of me, and sending me flying down the steps to impact hard with Uncle Gil.

Halstead's 'valet' walked right over both of us. Before I could stop seeing stars, he'd slung the bag into the truck and was roaring down the driveway, slewing and sliding before vanishing around a curve.

I straightened up and started to limp toward our hidden vehicle when my uncle grabbed my shoulder and croaked out, "No! Halstead!" He aimed me toward the front door and gave me a push.

I went through the front door, firearm ready, scanning right and left as I went. I had a bad feeling that I knew what

I would find, and as I entered a large open-space living room, I saw I was right. Lying writhing on the floor, the ex-county commissioner was desperately holding his stomach. I could see red between his fingers.

"Man down!" As I moved toward Halstead, I heard Uncle Gil coming in behind me, and a back door slamming open as Vinnie and Rosa entered from that side.

"Who're you?" Halstead gasped out.

"Bounty hunters, Mister Halstead," I told him as I pulled his hands away from the stomach wound giving him so much pain. A small round hole in his abdomen was leaking blood, and for a moment, I flashed back to a similar time I'd had to deal with something like this in a ritzy community on the shores of Lake Chelan.

"He.. That bastard.. He shot me!" Halstead gasped. "Bounty hunters? You're here after me... aren't you?"

"I think we're the least of your problems at the moment, sir," I told him as I reached for the trauma bandage that hung in a pouch on the side of my tactical vest. I covered the wound and applied just enough pressure to slow the bleeding. Halstead grunted with pain at the contact.

"Why did Cerrano shoot you?" Uncle Gil asked him.

Halstead looked at us with suspicion, but reality set in. He was screwed no matter what he did. He inferred that cooperation would ensure our help. He decided to come clean.

"I had a big duffel full of cash, almost a half million dollars. I have hidden accounts, but currently... didn't dare get in them. The cash was my emergency fund. I... knew things were getting dicey."

"And that was your bug-out fund."

"Yeah. Eduardo saw me putting it back in the duffel... and his eyes changed. One minute he was my guy, the next he pulled his gun on me and shot me without a word."

"Well, damn," I said. "He had a duffle over his shoulder

when he bowled us over. I'm guessing that's your cash." Halstead groaned, whether from the pain or the financial loss, I wasn't sure.

"Hello," Rosa was on Halstead's landline, "yes, Rosa Fernandez. I need to report a gunshot victim at..." she snapped her fingers at Uncle Gil who murmured something to her, "..8156 Lone Pine Road. Victim is conscious and we are applying first aid. We need an ambulance here, ASAP. Sheriff too."

She listened for a moment. "The victim is a fugitive who was shot by one of his accomplices, a man named Eduardo Cerrano. Cerrano has fled the scene and is driving a dusty white pickup..."

Uncle Gil leaned over and murmured at her again. Rosa continued; "A 2008 Ford F-150 with a canopy. License plate number GPV 210. Cerrano left the address at exactly 11:10 a.m. Yes, we saw him leave. He has a large amount of money with him and is armed and dangerous. Yes, we'll stay on scene, and continue to give first aid. All right, thanks."

"I'll take over here, Mac," Vinnie said. "Gil? Might be a good thing for humanity if you three went after Mr. Shoot-em-up. Guy like that shouldn't be roaming free."

I was kinda surprised at this. Vinnie, though he's like a brother to me, is not often the most altruistic person. We wouldn't get anything from going after Cerrano, other than a pat on the back from law enforcement. More likely we'd get cussed out for getting involved. Something about this event bothered our Vinn.

Uncle Gil looked at his business partner, at Vinnie's grim expression, and nodded. "Yeah, Vinn. Maybe this once we do some public service."

"Just bird dog him for the cops, Gil." He went back to applying pressure to Halstead's wound. "I'll make sure that Dick here doesn't fade away with our payday."

Rosa, Uncle Gil and I left the house and hot-footed it toward the war wagon. I couldn't help but notice that the gear from the back of the truck was lying on the driveway, having fallen out of the back of Cerrano's getaway vehicle. Rosa and I gave each other a covert look then detoured from our paths and each grabbed a brand-new backpack. Uncle Gil rolled his eyes.

"Leave 'em!" he said.

"Cerrano and Halstead aren't gonna be needin' them, Gilbert," Rosa said. "Shame to just leave them here in the dust..."

"Who knows?" I said, "We might need them as evidence later."

Uncle Gil rolled his eyes once more and continued on toward the truck. "They are part of the chain of evidence *here*. Part of the story for the cops. Leave 'em where they lie. Halstead will provide all the reward we get."

We ruefully left the gear behind.

———

We were getting close to the highway when we finally saw a sheriff's car go by us in the opposite direction, siren wailing, lights flashing. A few minutes later, an ambulance and an aid car went streaking past.

"The law is mobilized," I said. "We're likely wasting our time at this point."

"It's our time to waste," Uncle Gil replied. "Vinn's got the situation with Halstead locked down. Let's see if we can help the local law enforcement get a bead on Cerrano. I don't know about you, but someone who can turn on a dime like that and shoot someone isn't someone I want running loose in public."

"You can't put temptation in front of some people," Rosa

said. "Cerrano's the kind of guy who can go for years seeming like a semi-normal human, then when a big score lands in front of him, he'll do what he thinks he needs to without any warning. I knew people like this down in L.A. Honestly, Halstead should've kept his cash out of sight."

"Not so easy to do with that much physical money," Uncle Gil said. "Cerrano had to be suspicious of where Halstead was getting money to buy supplies with. And nothing screams "here's my large cash stash" like a big ol' zip-up duffel bag."

"You think Cerrano was planning on stealing it from the start?" I asked.

"It's speculation, but it seems likely," Uncle Gil said. "Cerrano proved to be a much more cold-blooded human being than his employer imagined him to be. It might've been purely impulsiveness to shoot, grab and run, but he sure didn't hesitate. And it was pure stupidity too."

"Yeah, I see what you're getting at," Rosa said. "They were obviously planning an overland trip to get across the border. Cerrano would've been better off waiting until they were out somewhere away from civilization and shooting Halstead there. Leave the body out in the woods."

"Yep. And remember that Cerrano wasn't a fugitive. If there was a crime before, it was simply aiding and abetting Halstead, but no one knew for sure they were together. He could've come back out of the woods, back to the USA with a big pile of free, unreported cash, and no one would've been the wiser."

"Some children have no impulse control," Rosa replied.

"I'd just bet that he's beating himself up about it now," I said. "In his position, I'd be telling myself that I should've just waited, and why didn't I wait." I was engaged in the speculation we'd been indulging in, but if you're in our business, half of what you do involves trying to think like a criminal.

Uncle Gil laughed. "You may be attributing more ability for self-introspection than Eduardo actually possesses."

It was just then, as we were about to pass a forest service road to our left, that the feeling hit me. It wasn't just a little intuitive tingle, my body literally jerked the wheel over into a slewing turn onto the dusty, graveled path.

19

"What the hell, Mac?" Uncle Gil yelled.

I didn't answer as I stepped out of the door. My mentor, Jim Three Feathers of the Okanogan's, was a shaman. I was not a shaman, but he'd been having me do a lot of exercises over the last few years to improve my intuition, and I was slowly learning to trust it. The more I trusted it, the more it seemed to very clearly tell me things. It had told me in no uncertain terms to turn onto the Forest Service road.

There was a patch of dusty road, where the gravel had evidently worn away over the years, and in that dust there were very fresh tire tracks. In my time as a tracker, I've worked for law enforcement a few times, and often trails have dead-ended at a set of tire tracks. Because of this, when on the job I have a tendency to mentally store the treads of tires that might be useful later. I'd done so with both Halstead's SUV and the dusty white F-150.

The tire tracks in the dust were from Cerrano's truck. I was sure.

As I stood, Uncle Gil came storming over. "Mac, what the hell are you doing?"

"He went this way."

"How can you be sure? This just seems like a random..."

"Mac's right, Gilbert," Rosa said. Instead of coming over to where we were, she'd walked back to the entrance to the fire road and was returning with a battered box in her arms. She pointed to it, and looking in, Uncle Gil and I saw some backpacking meals, a brand new first aid kit, still in plastic, and a tiny fold up stove.

"That had to have fallen out of the back of his pickup," she said.

Uncle Gil looked at me, one eyebrow raised and signaled for us to get back into the War Wagon. We took off, me driving, and perhaps driving a little faster than was safe.

We zoomed along through piney woods, throwing a large dust trail behind us. "He's using these back roads to avoid the highway," Rosa said. "Gil, where does this come out?"

"As far as I can tell," he replied, looking at a paper topographical map he'd bought specifically for Halstead's retrieval, "it forks here at this point. The right fork comes out near the main highway close to the border. The left fork goes west farther into the mountains, kinda paralleling the border. Its closest northerly point is about five miles from Canada."

"If I were him," I said, "that's the option I'd choose. Scoot through the woods."

"But he's not you, Mac," Uncle Gil said. "He's lost his supplies. That means he's not gonna have much with him except a duffle full of cash and a gun. I researched Cerrano a bit before this operation, and there's nothing in his profile to indicate he's anything other than a city boy."

"Yeah, but Canada is so close there. Anyone can walk five miles, even if it's overland."

"Says the kid that started practicing wilderness survival when he was twelve. Beyond the border, there's still a lot of forest that he'd have to navigate. Most people ain't you, kiddo. I'd bet dollars to doughnuts that Cerrano would look at all that deep forest, take stock of what he has, and give that left fork a hard no. My gut says he's sticking with his truck."

"Can we be sure?" Rosa asked.

"When we get to the fork in the road, we'll have Mac step out and look at the tire tracks, assuming it's not gravel." Uncle Gil replied.

"Not meaning to brag, Uncle Gil, but Cerrano's truck was the last thing driving on this road. Even if it's gravel, I'll be able to tell which way he turned just by looking at the dust on the gravel."

"Okay, then, as long as you're not bragging." We climbed into the SUV and continued the chase.

A strange thing has started to happen to me when I'm tracking. Occasionally, an oddity has happened as I track; something that my mentor, Jim Three Feathers, calls following the spirit trail. I will see a slight glow coming from the tracks, sometimes coalescing into connected streamers. It only happens once in a while, though Jim tells me that it will grow stronger the longer I track.

I started seeing what looked like a cyan afterimage on the road ahead, only it wasn't caused by any physical thing I'd seen. Ahead of us, two very faint glowing lines stretched out before us, eventually gaining the width of continuing tire tracks. Even with the gravel on the road, they were growing more and more obvious to me. Deep in my gut, I knew they were Cerrano's tracks. Jim had also told me that the closer I got to my objective, the more the glow would show. Something about energy dissipation.

It had happened before, so I hoped it happened this time when I really needed it.

When we came to the fork in the road, the trail went right, and I followed it without a moment's hesitation.

"I thought you were gonna stop and check the tracks," Uncle Gil said.

"He went this way."

"You sure?"

"I'm sure." I looked back at Rosa in the rear view mirror. "Woo woo stuff."

"Oh for Pete's sake, Mac," Uncle Gil said.

"You just have to face the facts, Gilbert," Rosa said. "Your nephew is a tracking *brujo*."

"Yeah? We'll see. Results matter."

We careened down the gravel road, the War Wagon occasionally slewing around when I took a turn on the switchbacked road too fast. As we progressed, the glowing tracks began to fade. At my awareness level, it was hard to maintain for any amount of time, but referring to the map, there were no other outlets between us and the highway.

When we finally reached the dirt road, I had to pull over and take a look at a muddy part of the ground to know for certain which way, right or left, that Cerrano had turned. Of course, Uncle Gil had to comment.

"What happened to your woo woo stuff?" he asked.

"I can't maintain it for very long yet. And it doesn't come very often."

"Well, that's not very helpful."

"I got us this far," I replied, trying to keep my voice even. "I've got his tire tracks. He turned toward the north, toward the border." I pointed at some traces of mud that still sat on the pavement.

Uncle Gil looked in the direction I had pointed. "Then let's get in and catch the sonuvabitch."

We pulled out onto the pavement in a slew of gravel, and I put our SUV up to the speed limit.

"I'd guess, if he has any brains at all," Rosa said, leaning forward between the front seats, "he'll keep at the speed limit. If he can slip across without tripping over the local sheriffs, he might even make it through the crossing if the local law hasn't had time to notify the Canadian border authorities."

"Mac, punch it," Uncle Gil said. "If we get a ticket, that's just the risk we'll have to take. He's only, maybe, ten minutes ahead of us. Let's make up the time."

Our War Wagon isn't just reinforced with bullet-proof panels and glass. The eight-cylinder 350 engine roared as we made like a missile down the road, and I passed a few speed-limit-maintaining cars like they were standing still.

"Gil!" Rosa said, pointing ahead, "There he is."

"We are entirely too close to the border." I said. "Can't be more than a few miles, now."

Cerrano's white pickup, canopy back open and tailgate still down, was less than half a mile ahead of us on the straight-away.

Uncle Gil pulled out his burner phone, and dialed 911. "Hello, yeah this is Gil Chambers. We were the people who called in the earlier gunshot wound. We are licensed fugitive retrieval officers. We're in pursuit of the assailant, and he is almost at the Canadian border on Highway 97. Do you have any officers nearby? We're... You do? Excellent! Can you let the deputy know that the suspect will be coming up on his position shortly? If he can roadblock Cerrano, my team can bottle him up from the rear. Great! We'll hang back a bit so we don't spook him."

"Don't get too close, Mac," He told me.

"Fly casually," Rosa said. She grinned and I rolled my eyes.

Cerrano drove on for the next two miles like a model citizen, even driving a few miles per hour under the speed limit. It took all of my self-control not to get any closer.

Our prey's casualness disappeared when an Okanogan County Sheriff's car dashed in front of him from a hidden spot along the highway. The deputy moved the car so that it blocked both lanes, and I saw that he'd chosen his ambush area well. Except for the side road he'd emerged from, there was a deep ditch along the highway on both sides. There'd be no going around the roadblock.

The only place to go was back, and as Cerrano's reverse lights came on, I threw the War Wagon crossways on the road behind him. He backed up a short ways, but seeing the Sheriff's car was the smaller vehicle, he put his truck's transmission in forward again and threw it at the car in front of him.

The deputy had already exited and was coming around to the other side of his car to use it as a shield. When he saw what Cerrano was up to, he bolted to the side, trying to avoid being smashed. He almost made it.

The white pickup slammed into the back end of the sheriff's car in an attempt to knock it aside. The spinning car caught the sheriff a glancing blow on the leg and he went flying into the ditch alongside the road. Cerrano might've gotten past at that point, except for modern safety devices. In the movies, the bad guy blows through the roadblock with nothing more than enough damage to his vehicle to look convincing.

In the real world, as Cerrano found out, there are these things called airbags.

If you've ever had one of these life-saving bits of technology go off in your face, you know it's a stunning experience, sometimes even putting car occupants into shock. Cerrano sat in the now stalling pickup, leaned back from the airbag, not moving. Rosa, Uncle Gil and I were out of our vehicle and moving forward immediately, weapons drawn and at the ready.

Cerrano, seemingly half-stunned, emerged from his now dead-in-the-water vehicle grabbing the door for support. As luck would have it, his own firearm slid out of the open door and, as is the cosmic way of things, bounced under the truck, fortunately not discharging as it hit the pavement. Cerrano started to bend down to retrieve it, nearly jumping out of his skin when Uncle Gil yelled at him.

"Cerrano! Back away from the vehicle! We've got you covered. You lay hands on that weapon and we'll all open fire!"

He evidently hadn't realized we were so close, jerking around and staring at us wide-eyed. He straightened, abandoning his attempts to get his weapon, and reached into the cab and pulled out the duffle. Spinning on his heel, he began to run/stagger toward the nearby trees.

'Mac, Rosa," Uncle Gil said, grinning, "Sic 'em."

Rosa and I could have shot Cerrano at any time, but putting a bullet into another human being, even one as reprehensible as Cerrano, isn't something anyone should do lightly. We holstered our Glocks, and I pulled out the extendible metal baton on my belt. Rosa grabbed her taser. We took off after our quarry at a dead run.

Wolves on the hunt.

Cerrano's head must've been clearing, because his gait steadied and his speed increased. Rosa and I, however, had passed out of our very sore stage and were in the best shape of our lives. We caught him less than fifty yards past the ditch.

Cerrano turned, using the duffle as a shield and pulled out a fast-open folding knife. Even though we were several feet away, he began slashing the air in front of him and cursing us in Spanish.

Rosa began yelling back at him in a fast-paced burst of the same language, the conversation going far too fast for my rudimentary Latin-language skills.

She circled to Cerrano's left, while I angled to his right,

thus splitting his attention between us. He was forced to keep his head on a swivel, trying to watch us both as we moved closer.

"Eduardo!" I yelled at him, trying to distract him. He turned briefly in my direction, then Rosa thumbed her taser. The electrical zapping sound, recognizable to anyone who's ever had a close call with electricity, jerked his head back toward her. I had my opportunity.

I leapt in as a fencer would, but instead of thrusting, I used one of Miyamoto Musashi's maxims: "rounding the corners." Rather than trying to hit Cerrano in the head or body, I brought the tip of the metal baton down on his forearm, just behind the wrist of his knife hand. Cerrano screamed, the knife went flying, Rosa jumped in with her taser.

Moments later, laying face down in the dirt, the still twitching man was cuffed behind his back. We pulled him up on shaky legs, and while Rosa brought the duffel and the knife, I none-too-gently maneuvered a staggering Eduardo Cerrano back to the waiting cars.

In the distance I could hear sirens approaching. The cars that had been stuck behind us on the highway began pulling to the shoulder giving the approaching deputies room to access the scene. Uncle Gil helped the deputy who'd formed the roadblock limp to his car. Both of them smiled to see Cerrano being manhandled back to the roadblock.

I couldn't help but grin back. I gave a thumbs-up, relieved to see that the officer had not been too seriously injured at the hands of this loser.

20

DevilKnight had talked her off the ledge. Collectively, they'd decided on a plan. She was calm, cool and collected now and she had methodology to get back in control of the situation.

She infiltrated the Uncle's farm, placing surveillance gear in multiple areas, some of them obvious, others almost impossible to find. She'd done the same for the girlfriend's apartment and the mother's house. She already had a listening device at MacKenzie's place.

Every vehicle they owned now had electronic tags, not the easy to spot commercial ones, but tiny, difficult to see, espionage grade versions Marjory had brought but never expected to need. Same with the target's business and its spare cars.

Even the wreck in the garage lot was double tagged.

"God knows I'd have that thing scrapped. Because I have class. Crow might think that vehicle is fine, looking like shit. But Crow is trailer trash.

He deserves to die.

And he will."

Young Crow would come back home eventually. Hopefully. And when he did, there would be another surprise waiting. She'd count coup once more and then get down to business. He couldn't come back without her knowing about it. Then, the final act would begin.

"I cannot wait to put the ending on this," she thought to herself. "When his bony ass hits the ground for the last time, I AM going to have my life back, and this little hiccup in my career will be a footnote rapidly receding in the rear view mirror."

She smiled to herself. "In the meantime, when he finds my little surprise, he should understand that his time is almost up."

21

I actually felt a little sorry for Janna. Sometimes it sucks to be the bail bond-person.

In the two days that it'd taken for Dick Halstead to be ambulanced down from Okanogan county, she must've had time to breathe both a sigh of relief she wouldn't have to be on the hook for Halstead's half million dollar bail, and to suffer the pain of the check she had to cut us for bringing him back.

I had to hand it to her, though. She handed over the envelope to Uncle Gil with barely a quiver. She even managed a shaky smile.

"You do good work, Gil," she said. "As painful as this payout is to my bottom line, it's an abject lesson on how far to trust someone. Fucking Halstead. I voted for him! I used to think he had some morals, that he might care about his reputation. I should'a known better."

"It's the high and mighty that are the least predictable, Janna," Uncle Gil told her. "Your street-level creep usually acts just the way you think they will. It's guys like Halstead that can seem like a stand-up guy most of their career only to turn out to be rotten at their core if someone digs deep."

"Yeah," she replied tightly, "lesson learned. Now, if you'll excuse me, I think I'll go visit the former commissioner in his hospital room, and tell him what a miserable excuse for a human being he is."

"Good. I'm sure that'll be just the medicine he needs and deserves."

After stopping by our local bank (Gil Chambers Rule # 2: Always deposit the check as quickly as possible), he took us all out to lunch as was the custom after a successful hunt. We wound up at the "Fire Pizza" shop in the Pybus Market, down by the riverfront.

Sitting out in the fall sunshine, it was an ideal day. Perfect temperature, blues skies... and wide open. This should have been a great time: successful hunt, big team payout, perfect weather, good pizza. But I found myself looking around constantly, hyper-vigilant, worrying that we were being watched by someone sinister. I noticed Rosa was doing the same. Vinnie noticed us both.

"You two look like cats locked in the dog pound," he said.

"Wouldn't you be?" Rosa said. "Mac's got a target painted on his back. That we were successful with Halstead doesn't change that."

"Maybe not," Uncle Gil said. "But life is short. Don't let this low-life drain all color out of it, Rosa. But since we're here and I chose this outdoor table for the ambient noise, maybe we should start discussing a way to flush this creep."

"Seems to me that the only way to do that, is to offer up some bait," I said. "I think we all know who the bait would have to be."

"No!" Rosa said, some heat in her voice. "That is not acceptable."

"Agreed," Uncle Gil replied. "But maybe we can use the promise of Mac to lure our psycho in."

"Meaning?" Vinnie asked.

"We make sure he knows that Mac is back in the area. Then, we take Mac's phone, retrieved from the post office, and move it to Mac's trailer. We have a very skilled sniper up top." He gestured toward Vinnie. "While the rest of us wait for our prey in various points near the trailer, well-hidden of course. Often it's the hunter who knows where to wait that gets the deer, as opposed to the one who searches all over the country sides."

"Gonna be hard to explain sniping someone to the cops," Vinnie said. "I don't like the idea of winding up in Monroe State Penitentiary."

"You only have to shoot if things go bad, Vinn. It's been made abundantly clear to the cops that Mac has someone after him. You'd only fire if one of us was down. That might be a little tricky legally, but if we can prove homicidal criminal intent, then we can spin it to self-defense."

"Yeeah... no." Vinnie shook his head. "I'm not too comfortable with doing war-time stuff in a civilian situation. Understand, I'd have no qualms about putting a mad dog down, 'specially if they've hurt one of the family, but this is gonna look bad to the cops any way you want to spin it."

"Well," Rosa said, lowering her voice, "if there's a body, there's a nice big river right there."

"Let's not ride that train of thought too far," I said. "We're the good guys, remember."

"If it means keeping my family safe," Rosa replied, her voice tight with emotion, "I am willing to be a very bad girl. Never doubt it."

"Our goal, remember, would be to capture, not kill," Uncle Gil said. "Lethal force is always our last resort." He looked around at the lunch crowd which was beginning to filter in around us and leaned forward, speaking softly. "Guys, maybe this wasn't a good place to come. Let's box up our pizza. I think if we're going to discuss this, we should do it a little less publicly. Out at the farm."

———

We pulled into the dusty driveway of the farm around two p.m. As we drove up, Ed Burnbaum walked over from the remodeled bunkhouse.

"Hail, conquering heroes! What's the news from far-off lands?" he asked.

"Success, my lord," I replied. "The Britons will surely become part of the empire soon. Also, Commissioner Dick Halstead is in custody."

"Also," Rosa said. "We no longer trust our phones."

Ed blinked at that. "Not that I ever thought smartphones and all that comes with them are trustworthy, but I never thought I'd hear you young people speak such a blasphemy."

"We think Mac's stalker might've been using his phone to keep tabs on him and maybe Rosa too. Maybe all of us." Uncle Gil told him. "We mailed them to the office while we were on the road."

Ed looked off down the driveway then turned back to my uncle. "I guess that's why my call to you went to voice mail."

"Something urgent?" Vinnie asked. "You usually don't call us on a job 'less it's an emergency, Ed."

"Yeah, somethin.' Went out on the porch to drink a cup o' coffee and watch the sunrise, as I customarily do, and saw tracks in the morning dew on the grass. If I'd emerged an hour later, things might've dried out enough I wouldn't have thought to look. But at that hour, there's enough dew on the grass that even Mel could see 'em."

Ed was my original Yoda, continuing my training in

tracking after I'd been expelled from the Seeker School as a teenager. If he said there were tracks to be mindful of, all of us knew to listen closely.

"You follow 'em?" Vinnie asked.

Ed gave him a flat look in return.

"Of course you did. Sorry Ed. What'd you find?"

"They came to the house through the sagebrush," he said, gesturing toward the sea of the stuff between here and the road. The previous owner had wanted the view from front his porch to be natural, as opposed to the fields out back which were currently filled with young grape vines. "I guess they must've had some track consciousness to not come down the driveway in the dust, but to a real tracker, once I knew someone had been here, it wasn't that hard to follow their trail."

"We should check the security camera footage," Rosa said. "It'll show us who it was, even if it was dark."

"Already did that, M'dear. About two a.m., the mercury vapor light on the side of the bunkhouse went out, and a few seconds later, the feeds from each of the security cams goes dark. One at a time. I'm no electronics expert, but the cameras themselves look to be burnt out somehow."

"Shit. Did you get anything from the tracks as to where they went while they were here? Or where they walked in from?" I asked.

"She walked in from about a half mile down the road," Ed said "And..."

"She?" Vinnie said.

"She was wearing men's boots, but in a few places, you could see where her foot rolled sideways from too loose footwear. Also, the width of the trail, the slight toeing in and width distance between the feet said to me the owner was female, even if she was trying to pull a fast one. Hard to hide wide hips, and this one likely has a very womanly figure."

"I'll take your word for it, Ed," Uncle Gil said. "The attack on our security system says to me this isn't some random nut job with a hate on for Mac. This is pro-level infiltration. My guess is that we're bugged seven ways to Sunday, and until I can get a professional of my acquaintance out here to fumigate the place, we need to operate as if this farm is compromised in every way."

"Yeah, Gil?" Ed said. "I actually sent the girls off to a hotel already. See, there's one more thing, and it's a big one." He gestured toward Rosa's RAV.

"Oh Christ, what now, Ed?" I said.

"Mac, you and Rosa stay with your War Wagon there. In fact, why don't you, Rosa and Vinn take a step behind it. Gil, come take a look."

Rosa, Vinnie and I watched as the two older men looked into the driver's seat of the Toyota. Uncle Gil stared at what he was seeing there for a moment, then, slowly he lowered himself to look underneath the vehicle. We heard his gasp and quiet curse from twenty yards away.

Normally, Uncle Gil gets up a little stiffly, being in his mid-fifties. This time he sprang back up to standing with all the quickness of a twenty-year-old on speed. He and Ed walked back toward us with purpose in their stride.

"What is it, Gilbert?" Rosa asked.

"There's one of her little calling cards, folded tent-like in the seat. The words are written in black sharpie so you can see them easily. It says 'look underneath,' with a little joker face below the grim reaper art."

"What'd you find under the Rav?" Vinnie asked. "Though I think I already guessed."

"If you guessed a bomb, Vinn, then you guessed right," Ed said. "Looks like a pipe bomb of some sort with a little antenna sticking out."

We all inadvertently took a step farther behind the War Wagon.

"All right," Uncle Gil said, with all the bearing of the military captain he used to be, "Ed, I want you to call the local sheriff department and tell them the situation. Let's get a bomb squad out here as fast as we flippin' can. We need experts. Vinnie, as soon as Ed's done, I want you both to sweep the area and look for anything else suspicious."

"Yeah, bombs are pretty suspicious," Vinnie said.

"Why would she warn us?" Rosa asked.

"It's like she's playing a game," I said.

"And we don't know what her game is," Uncle Gil said, looking back at the RAV. "Let's make sure this is the only bomb. I know we weren't staying at any hotels on this last trip, Vinn, but did you happen to bring the 'camera sniffer' we use to make sure there aren't hidden video devices in our hotel rooms?"

"Yeah, I always bring that sort of thing, Gil. I'll take it with me when I sweep and see if I can find any hidden surveillance crap."

"Sweep the interior of the buildings too. If our friend is this good, I'd guess she's probably an expert at lock picking also. Since Ed and Mel live in the bunkhouse, this person likely had free rein of my house."

Uncle Gil turned to Rosa and I. "You two, with me. We're going to take a little hike in the canyon."

———

The "Canyon" behind the ranch is one of my favorite places. Once you leave the fields, it's just a ways over some small hills to hit the narrow valley a large creek flows through. The creek is a meandering oasis surrounded by brown hills and sage brush

Every fifty yards or so, there's a beaver dam, and this continues almost all the way out to the Palisades coulee. The large beaver population's handiwork has allowed the growth of all sorts of greenery including trees, grasses and shrubs. There's wildlife everywhere near the water.

Unfortunately, I wasn't really seeing any of it as I walked down the broken dirt road that parallels the creek. I was thinking about what would've happened if Rosa and I had been in her RAV when she started it.

We were at an area where the creek narrowed, with numerous basalt rocks around it, when Uncle Gil signaled a halt.

"Let's sit here. The noise of the creek will cover everything we say."

"You think someone might be listening out here?" Rosa asked.

"Probably not. But my level of paranoia has been raised to DEFCOM 1, which is saying something. Cutting to the chase, you two need to leave. For parts unknown. As soon as we can get you out of here."

"We're running?" I said.

"You're getting out of harm's way, kiddo," Uncle Gil said. "I want you both to be hard to find until we can get a handle on who's doing this. I'm gonna contact Steve Hanger. He's living down in Florida now, and we all know how good he is at certain... under the radar activities. I have a couple unused burner phones, I'm giving one to Rosa, and I'll give that number to Steve."

"In the meantime," I said, "Rosa and I have to get to Florida undetected. If this person is as connected as we're starting to think, they might be able to track us if we fly," I said.

"You two wait out here," Uncle Gil replied. "I need to get

some things from the house." He took off back the way we'd come.

"Wow. Looks like we get an unplanned vacation to Florida," Rosa said. "Though damned if I know how we're going to get there."

"If we had a good chunk of cash, I guess we could hitch down. Be pretty hard to trace us then."

"Ugh. I've done enough of that in my life to know it can really suck, Mac. Especially when you get out into places like Wyoming or Colorado. Not to mention, winter's not that far off."

"I'm not thrilled with the idea, either," I said. "But I'm less thrilled with the idea of being blown up."

"If we can get to Florida, though, there's no one I trust more to get us hidden than Steve Hanger. He helped save our bacon when those mercenaries came after us."

Steve was a military contemporary of Uncle Gil's, and they'd been friends for a long time. My uncle hinted that they'd done some off-the-books things together for the government.

We were still hashing and rehashing ideas when Uncle Gil showed back up. He had a medium-sized black backpack over each shoulder. He handed one to Rosa, and one to me.

"Where'd these come from?" Rosa asked him.

"That one there," he said, pointing to the backpack I held, "is my Get Outta Dodge bag. The one you're holding is Mel's. You may want to buy different clothes on the way, as Mel's about 6 inches shorter and 50 pounds heavier than you, Rosa. Mac might need to roll up the pant legs and sleeves of my bug out clothes."

"We've both got Go-bags that we've already filled with our own stuff, Uncle Gil."

"Uh huh. Funny, I don't see 'em, Mac."

"Well, mine's back at my trailer and... Okay. I see your point."

"Even if we'd had them along in the Rav," Rosa said, "we couldn't really safely access them. Shit."

"You'll be able to buy clothes, and whatever else you might be missing along the way," Uncle Gil said.

"Where we gonna go with these?" I asked. "Rosa and I were talking about hitchhiking to Florida, but do we need to leave right this minute?"

"'Fraid so, Mac, or perhaps I should say Lucas."

"*Que?*" Rosa asked, as confused as I was.

"I will explain, Carmen," he said, eliciting a confused look from both of us. He handed each of us a thick envelope. Opening mine, I found a passport, a credit card and a government issued ID card, along with five thousand in cash in fifties and hundreds. The passport and ID both had my face, and the name Lucas McClintock. The credit card had the same name.

"Carmen Alvarez?" Rosa said, looking at her documents. "Gilbert. Are you telling me you had all these false ID's and credit cards all ready to go? What were you expecting? For us all to need to go anonymous? Gil, that's some next-level paranoia."

"And yet, Ms. Fernandez, here we are. Maybe not so paranoid as you think. There are packets just like this for all of us. Me, Ed and Mel, as well as your mom. Bug-out bags prepared for the whole family. I'd have one for Vinnie, but I know he's already built one of his own."

"I guess that makes sense..." Rosa started looking through her pack.

"If things fall apart in this country, as I worry that they might," Uncle Gil continued, "we can be on our way to Alaska to a little island with a nice lodge on it, just a ways out from Ketchikan. The fishing is great there.

"Why is this the first time I'm hearing about it?" I asked.

"I could go into more detail about how I maintain these things, but we don't really have time. Everything I just gave you will stand up to all but the deepest scrutiny. The credit cards just need to be activated."

Rosa and I stared at him. There were a lot of mysteries about my uncle, and his time working for the government, but now it seemed like we really didn't know very much about him at all.

"All right. Now that I have your attention," he said, "let's talk strategy. You will need to do a little hitch-hiking, but only as far as Quincy. Hike out to the end of the canyon here to the Palisades coulee, then, either there or on Highway 28, catch a ride to Quincy. From there, a friend of mine will give you a ride to Spokane. Then, and only then, will you use these credit cards and IDs. Spokane is far enough away that I'm pretty sure you can fly out without causing any alarms. And for God's sake, look as innocent as possible. You get into any kinda situation with TSA and they might fingerprint you, then our house of cards comes tumbling down."

"Where are we flying to?" Rosa asked. "Florida, I got. But where in Florida?"

"Steve lives in Bradenton, near Tampa. He'll pick you up at the Tampa airport." Uncle Gil handed Rosa an unopened burner phone. "Don't even think of using this until you're in Florida. Never call home; relay everything through Steve. We want you to disappear as completely as civilians ever can in this high-tech society."

22

"Oh God, that was great!"

Of course, Marjory'd set one of her cameras to watch the RAV, and the show when they'd arrived back at the ranch house hadn't disappointed. The white faces they'd had when they found the bomb were worth all the effort she'd expended to bug the house.

She'd enjoyed that reaction all out of proportion to what satisfaction she'd expected to feel. It was almost a shame to bring this assignment to a close. She hadn't gotten this much of a thrill out of her job in years. Always, she'd had to live by the Association's creed, "Get in, get it done, get out without being seen." This was like her early days, before Timothy had sponsored her. She missed that wildness and innovation, but she didn't miss the lousy payouts.

Now, the main question was whether to finish the kid with style, or brutal efficiency. She was leaning toward efficiency, she'd more than proven that she could conduct a psy-op.

It was time to end this. Time to finish the kid and take all her notes and reports back to the Association and hope it'd be enough for them to take her back. Certainly, they'd see she could think on her feet and reinstate her.

If they didn't, she'd have to take what little money she'd held back *and take a page from what could've been young Crow's book. Slide into Canada, somewhere remote and work real hard on becoming anonymous, untraceable.*

If they didn't take her back, they'd want to retire her. Most likely with a 9mm double tap to the back of the skull.

She had no intention of going quietly into that long night.

23

Getting to Spokane went smoothly.

The ten-mile hike to the highway was easy compared to the trail running we'd been doing. We caught a ride at a small mini-market across Highway 28 from the Palisades road which took us to the small farming community of Quincy, Washington. All very under the radar.

At the Quincy McDonalds, Gonzalo, Uncle Gil's friend, picked us up and drove us the three hours to Spokane, dropping us off at the airport. During the entire trip, he said maybe three words. Even when Rosa tried to engage him in Spanish, he mostly just stayed with mono-syllables. I was sure it wasn't because he was unable to converse with us, he just didn't want to talk. Nonetheless, we were grateful for the ride and tried to give him some cash but he waved it away, saying: "No. Paying old debts."

As we entered the terminal, the burner phone Rosa carried chimed. There was a text from an out of state number that read, *"Lucas, Carmen, two tickets ready for you, Alaska flight 1745, leaving 5:45 your time."*

Rosa showed me the text. "Who do you think sent this?" she asked. "Gilbert or Steve? The numbers are hidden."

"If they're first class tickets, then I'd say Steve. If we're flying economy, I'm guessing Uncle Gil." Rosa solemnly nodded in agreement.

We were several hours ahead of schedule, so we went to a semi-secluded corner to go over what was in the backpacks. Aside from clothes, there were all the survival items that you might need, including knives and multi-tools, even some metal cookware. The bags hadn't been intended to get through TSA security lines apparently.

A quick look at the clothes in her bag sent Rosa to one of the stores on the exterior of the airport to get a traveling outfit. I was able to fit into Uncle Gil's clothes, just rolling up sleeves and cuffs. I changed out of my black, paramilitary work clothes, and into "civvies."

Rosa returned from the store, dressed in a tight-fitting long-sleeved blue blouse with intricate artwork that expounded upon the love of coffee. She wore black form-fitting pants, and a new pair of wool topped tennis shoes. To say she looked gorgeous would be like saying the Mona Lisa is a painting. True, but falling far short of the whole story and well into the territory of understatement.

As I often did, I marveled that this incredible woman had seen fit to be involved with me. It was amazing, but I sure wasn't going to say anything to jinx it.

"Mac, come over here," Rosa gestured toward the store she'd just purchased her clothing from. She pointed to a couple of close-body sling bags. "Let's get these for our cash and a few items to take on board. I think it would be wise to check the backpacks at the counter, don't you?" I agreed.

Our burner was not a smartphone. It was a flipper with texting capabilities. It's amazing how much we've come to rely on our modern personal cell phones. We could've just walked over to the Kiosks, checked in electronically and used the ticket's QR code to get on the plane. Instead, waiting in line for twenty minutes, we had to approach an agent and test out our new IDs. They turned out to be as good as Uncle Gil had claimed, and we walked away without packs and with printed boarding passes.

The second test was the security line. This was the biggie. If we were caught trying to board with false identities, we'd be in a world of hurt.

"Mac, calm your expression," Rosa said. "Never look guilty. Always look natural."

"Easier said than done," I replied. Rosa could smile and look nonchalant with ease. I, on the other hand, was one of the world's worst liars. Rosa often said I wore my heart on my face, not my sleeve.

Rosa was as cool as a cucumber when she handed her boarding pass and ID to the agent. He glanced at it, scanned it and said, "Next."

I've always hated security screenings. I'm not a terrorist. I'm not a criminal and I have no nefarious plans, but TSA always makes me nervous. This time, I used every mind-calming technique that Sensei Uchida had been trying to teach me. Evidently, they worked. Or I just got lucky.

The agent looked at my stuff, looked at me and spoke the glorious word; "Next."

As we were carrying very little we breezed through the screening and found ourselves putting our shoes back on in the post-security section of the terminal.

A few hours later, after an overpriced meal in the terminal, we were on a plane to Florida.

———

Tampa International Airport is damn big.

Having flown east into later and later time zones, it was growing dark by the time our flight touched down. Having risen from bed at 3:00 a.m the previous morning, we both felt as mentally acute as road-killed raccoons.

Rosa and I, after stiffly climbing out of our near-the-back-of-the-plane economy seats, were not at our best. We'd talked to each other for half the trip, but our desire to not discuss our current situation while the person in the aisle seat was awake had limited our conversation.

Neither of us had had the forethought to buy a book before we boarded. Usually, I read books on my phone, while Rosa liked to listen to podcasts. Our single flip-phone offered none of these options. After exhausting conversation about what future plans we'd like to indulge in, including maybe building a small house where my Airstream currently sat, I'd been forced to try meditation/sleeping. Rosa had watched one of the Marvel movies on a tiny pay-for-play device rented from the airline.

Shortly after arriving, the burner chimed with another text; *"I'll pick you up at the Uber area. Red Toyota Highlander. See you then, S."*

Normally, we'd have checked our phones to find where we were going, but practically being analog, we had to ask. It's amazing how people can work at an airport, and not know where anything is. We had to ask no less than three airport employees before we received coherent directions. We walked to the other end of the airport, past a huge, two-story art-flamingo, and eventually began to see signs that led where we needed to go.

The red Toyota was sitting at a curb, along with a number of other cars picking up arriving passengers. Before we even reached it, the rear hatch door popped open and a tall, gaunt man of my uncle's age stepped forward to greet us. Steve Hanger, trying to blend in with all the 'normal' people stood out a bit. Even his body language seemed to say "ready for anything."

He seemed a bit surprised when Rosa threw her arms around him.

"Thank you, Steve," she said. "Thank you for coming to our rescue."

"Ah.. Well," he said. "We've all been through a small war together, haven't we? Least I could do for your family. Let's get out of this crazy ol' airport and head for my house. We can talk about how things are going to go when we get there. Also, I have presents. From what Gil told me, these'll make you two very happy."

He held up two iPhones. Rosa had hers in her hand with all the speed of a striking snake.

"These are your Florida phones," Steve told us. "They're through a shell business I own. My number is in each. Needless to say, you dare not log in to any of your social media, email, or accounts of any kind, or they'll be linked to you. Do not call, text, FaceTime or in any way use them to contact home. You contact me. I have ways of getting in touch with Gil that are below the standard radar. Use these for contacting me, news, internet, GPS, and calling each other, but as I said before, do not log into any account you currently have. Clear?"

"Crystal clear," I said. "As Rosa said, thanks for saving our bacon."

"It helps pass the time," he said, a slight smile on his face. "Let's get you to my house. I'll bet you're both ready to hit the hay."

"Truer words were never spoken."

24

It isn't time to panic. At least, not yet.

Chambers, the old man, was a lot more savvy than Marjory had figured. He'd returned from wherever they'd gone without MacKenzie or the woman, Rosa. Marjory figured they'd been picked up away from the scene of the bomb and taken elsewhere.

A day later, a man came to the farm and the bastard found eighty percent of her devices. He'd also done the same at all of the other places she'd left gear.

Expensive gear at that. All now lost. She'd had no idea that Chambers had access to that level of technical assistance.

A few of her best, most covert devices were still in action though, and she was sure the two young people hadn't returned to the farm. Nor had they gone to the girlfriend, Rosa's, apartment. Nor the mother's house.

And especially not back to MacKenzie's trailer.

"Not panicking," she thought, lighting a cigarette and blowing the calming smoke off the balcony of the AirBNB she was currently staying in. "But what if the little fucker's gone to ground out in the mountains somewhere?" It was October now, and from everything she'd learned, it could start snowing within a few weeks. She couldn't

believe that any sane person would be hardcore enough to take camping gear and brave the heavy snows around here.

Marjory had enough information gathering skills to access the public records for the county. The uncle owned a tiny cabin up at a huge lake to the North, Lake Chelan. It was sequestered in a little isolated town at the far end. Steheikin, only reachable by a four-hour ferry ride. Or the Pacific Crest Trail. Either way, this seemed the likely hideaway spot.

She'd purchased a ticket for the ferry, made a reservation at a local AirBnB, loaded her gear and headed for Chelan. Hopefully this cabin was far enough away from any others that a silenced pistol shot wouldn't be noticed.

25

The next morning, I awoke groggy but fairly well rested. Looking to the other side of the bed, I saw Rosa had gotten up without waking me. Swinging my legs onto the thankfully carpeted floor, I blundered into the bathroom for a quick shower.

Feeling much more human when I emerged, I dressed and went looking for the other two-legged creatures staying here. On the way, I found a fresh pot of coffee, and poured a cup into a mug that read 'Raven Coffee Company, Quoth the raven, Nevermore.' A small but skilled drawing of a raven sat above the quote. Some might've considered that a bad omen, but I knew and loved ravens. Always a good omen, in my opinion.

I found Steve and Rosa sitting on a screened-in patio with a small pool. Rosa looked at me as I wandered out, rewarding me with her thousand-watt smile. Steve enigmatically kept staring out at his backyard vista.

"Nice view," I said. The back yard led right down to what looked like a man-made lake. An Osprey flew over, looking for breakfast. It was a decidedly middle-class neighborhood, but the developers had planned it so that most of the homes had a view of the water from their patios.

"Pull up a lawn chair, Mac," Steve said, gesturing to a stack of such chairs in the corner. "We can take a few moments to discuss the general strategy I've worked out for keeping you two under the radar."

"Steve thinks we need to keep on the move," Rosa told me as I sat in the slightly dusty chair.

"Really?" I asked. "I mean we've switched identities, hoofed it overland, hitch hiked and then flown to Florida under fake IDs. I don't even think Gladys, for all her web wizardry, could find us at this point." Gladys, and her hacker-for-hire information services were nothing short of miracle workers when it came to ferreting out information. It was a bold statement to make, but I felt good about it.

Rosa gave me the all-knowing eyebrow and shook her head.

Don't jinx us, goofball.

"You've done pretty well, but..." he said, eyeing us both. "This info is not to be shared, but I do a fair amount of work for the CIA still. You'd be amazed at what they can do. A good portion of America is now wired into a surveillance network of private, business and municipal cameras. Even small towns are starting to become part of the network these days. Bottom line is, if you're in civilization and the CIA is looking for you, facial recognition software has gotten to the point that you'll eventually be identified."

"But that's upper level intelligence stuff, isn't it?" Rosa asked.

"Much of that info is accessible to local law enforcement. I assure you, there are hackers on the Dark Web that can very likely program a search for you and use the government's systems to find you. They don't access it through trying to hack into federal computers, they go in through a sheriff's office in Big Fart, Montana, and use that access to get into the larger networks. So, it's going to be hats and sunglasses for you both whenever you leave wherever you happen to be staying. And Mac? Start growing a beard. Also, you're both going to be holdovers from Covid and wear masks when going out in public."

We sat there silently for a few moments digesting this information. It wasn't just the fact that it was possible to track us after all these exceptional efforts to go under the radar, it was the fact that America was rapidly becoming a surveillance state that even the old USSR would've been amazed at. What's worse, the thought that skilled hackers could use that network was terrifying in its own way.

"Well, fuck," Rosa said.

"That's a good summation," Steve replied. "The good news is that I truly believe that is the only problem point in the plan. I have a small SUV belonging to the business that you can use to keep mobile. With caution and proper phone discipline we can keep you out of trouble until Gil, myself and a friend in the agency can isolate who's targeting you."

"In the meantime," I said. "You have an itinerary to keep us moving. Will we be able to go out of the house?"

"With the precautions I've outlined, you can probably go to, say, a Walmart and get supplies. Maybe take a "stay sane" trip out to some of the state parks. I'd avoid moving around in urban areas very much simply due to greater density of surveillance cameras."

"Well, alright then," Rosa said. "I guess we have an idea of what we're up against. Let's hear this itinerary you've come up with for us."

We'd driven to Steve's home in the dark. Even though a major city like Tampa has street lights everywhere, I'd still not gotten a real "lay-of-the-land" on our way in. Now, with Rosa driving the spare car and me playing navigator, I was starting to realize one main thing about the Sunshine State.

It was flat as a dime.

The Honda CRV Steve had loaned us was fairly new, with a fancy onboard view screen system aiding in a number of things, even backing up. Very space age to a luddite like myself who owned a car that Rent-a-Wreck would've turned their nose up at.

When driving along, a small annotation in the upper left corner of the screen gave us the distance above sea level. Five feet. Eight feet. Three feet. My trailer back in Washington, sunk down in the Columbia Gorge, was at roughly a thousand feet above sea level.

I was used to mountains and trees. Sure there was beautiful blue ocean – and alligators, sharks, and mosquitos if the truth be told - but not much in the landscape department that I could see. At least Kauai had cliffs and waterfalls. Here in Florida it was sky and horizon.

"Even if a hurricane misses this area," I said. "I wouldn't be surprised if the whole place floods in a hard rain storm. Floods with salt water." Rosa didn't respond. I glanced over at her. She was staring out the windshield, deep in thought. When she began speaking, it had nothing to do with altitude.

"I've been trying to figure this out," She said. "The thing is, Mac, in the grand scheme of things, you're just not that important."

"And I thought you cared," I replied, assuming a slightly pompous air.

She continued, without the slightest nod at my attempt at humor, "You're very important to me, to our family, to our friends, but on the larger stage, you and I are just part of the teeming masses. I was wondering if this whole thing isn't maybe government sponsored, but that just makes no sense."

"Maybe...?"

"Aside from Gil's paranoia that the government is out to get us, I don't really believe all the movie crap that the United States three-letter agencies are willing to assassinate U.S. Citizens," Rosa added.

"Not without a good reason," I interjected. "Not just for shits and giggles. Waste of resources."

Rosa shrugged. "It looks good in a screenplay, but I find it pretty hard to swallow in real life."

"Yeah? Why?" I asked.

"You have to ask yourself, 'who is benefitting from channeling your fear into this wild story of your own government going after you?' Most likely someone who is in the status quo who wants to keep the masses docile, the brown people under their boots, and the money and power for themselves." Rosa frowned. "Even school children in other countries are taught how to spot these tactics."

"I guess we Americans are particularly gullible. So what does that have to do with us? All I can say is it's a damn good thing we had bug-out bags already made! Oh, turn left at the next light."

She did so and continued. "But whoever is after us seems like they might have a lot of resources to bring to bear. Civilian operators who can track your phone? Being able to hack into the nationwide surveillance camera net? They're operating at a big-league level."

"I'd point out that we have no idea if they can actually hack those cameras. We're just speculating on that."

"Well I'm certainly not willing to take a chance on it, Mac. Are you?"

"That's a big nope. We follow Hiding Master Steve's teachings to the letter." We turned off into a sizable parking lot, with a large sign reading, "Robinson Preserve." We left the CRV in the parking lot, and shouldering our sling bags, we headed out along an asphalted trail, along with several other tourists and local park goers. The farther out we went, the thinner the crowds became, until eventually we made a stop at what looked like a fire tower. Climbing to the top, Rosa continued her train of thought.

"There are murders all the time, but it's usually someone's pissed off lover. Or someone owes someone money."

"Hey, don't look at me! You're the only one for me, and hopefully I haven't pissed you off *that* much. As far as I know, the only debt of any size I owe is to the bank for my mortgage."

"Even hypothetically," she said, "if I was that angry with you that I went crazy and wanted you dead, I'd have no idea where to find someone of *this caliber* to kill you. Few Americans, or for that matter any normal citizen of most countries, would have any idea how to do that."

"Geez, I sure hope not. Even most of the people we've helped put behind bars are no way at this level of expertise."

"From what I understand," Rosa said, "most murders for hire are done by low-level criminals, none of whom could even approach this level of technical... excellence."

"No" I replied. "This is definitely several levels above your average killer for hire."

"The only logical conclusion is that someone with a lot of money, power, and balls decided you need to die. For the life of me, I just can't figure who that would be. You don't exactly run in the same circles as the power elite."

"There's only one guy with that kind of power that I've pissed off enough for them to want me dead. And he died in prison several years ago. Almost as soon as he was incarcerated."

"Dallum."

"Yep," I replied. "Charles P. Dallum. Socialite sociopath. Progenitor of psychopaths. My first big case, and, I might add, dead as a doornail."

"He did send mercenaries after us."

"Well, yeah. But I'll remind you that he was alive at that time. Much easier to hire your murders done while you're still breathing."

Rosa acted as if she was considering that statement. "Hmmmm. That does kinda put him out of the running. I guess if ol' Chuck wanted to hire it done, he'd have engaged someone before or just after his trial."

"It's been a number of years, now. Dallum didn't seem like the kinda guy who'd wait for delayed gratification." I looked her directly in the eye. "Hey, Rosa?"

"Yeah?"

"Thank you." I felt my throat tightening up with emotion. "Thank you for coming with me and having my back. I've somehow put you in danger and there is nothing about this whole situation that weighs on me more heavily than that. I should've come on this trip by myself."

I was unprepared for the fierce look she aimed my way. Rosa reached up and grabbed my lower lip.

"Now you listen to me, Mac. I love you. Whether it's sunk in or not, someday I intend to marry you, maybe have babies with you. That won't happen if I let some punk-ass assassin kill you. I've got to protect my investment," she said. "Besides, the bitch put a bomb under *my* car. For all we know, this hit is a package deal, so no more of that talk. We protect each other, *comprender?*"

"Understood." I said, my mind whirling with her declarations. A slow involuntary grin began to spread over my face. "Maybe we should move in together when this is over."

"Oh Mac, I'm sure you don't want to live in my apartment and leave your little oasis. And there's no way I'm moving into that tiny-ass trailer. Let's talk when you get something bigger put in out there."

"Okay," I said, my mind already beginning to brainstorm ways to add more living space to my property.

From the tower, we looked out over the preserve. To one side, I could see massive bridges gracefully curving over large bodies of what I assumed were salt water. I'd guess the everyday commuter would just see them as utilitarian byways, but as a tourist, I found them to be like something out of a science fiction novel. As an admitted nature boy, it was rare that I was impressed by man-made structures, but these flowing graceful bridges, seemingly driving across open ocean, left me in awe.

"Shall we get a run in, Mac?"

"Could we do the circuit trail at a walk for the first lap? This is so different from the bio-regions I'm used to, I'd kinda like a little time to get to know it."

Rosa had no objection. As we walked, I mentally became more in tune with the preserve. Ospreys flew overhead regularly, and seemed to be everywhere. Back home, you might see the occasional osprey near a river or lake, but it was a special surprise when you did. Here, I seemed to see one every five minutes.

Like a letter from home, I saw raccoon tracks cross the trail. A youngish female followed by two kits. They were small enough that I wondered if the mother had lost a first litter and had gotten pregnant a second time. Usually, by October, the young ones were a bit bigger. Of course down here, the mother didn't have to worry about a hard winter. Just the occasional hurricane.

We finally worked our way back to the car, dropped off our water bottles and stretched a little to get the blood flowing. We started the beginning of the loop at a leisurely pace, picking up speed and dodging walkers as we went. We got a few dirty looks from some birdwatchers, but we were past them so fast neither side had time to get salty.

Five or so miles later, we sweatily arrived back at the parking lot. I'd sweated a lot more than I expected, and went right for my water. Somehow, Rosa only had a tiny bit of perspiration at her neckline. Some sort of strange magic gift from her Mexican ancestors I guessed. My ancestors were more lined up with wet and cold, not heat and humidity.

"Geez it's hot," I said. "Was not expecting to drown in my own sweat."

"*Pobre bebé*," Rosa said. "Did my northern boy not expect the South would be hot?"

"Hey. It gets very hot during the summer at home. I just wasn't expecting this sort of warmth in October."

"Changes in attitude, changes in latitude..."

"I guess so."

"Can we make a few stops on the way back to Steve's?" Rosa said. "Quite frankly, Mel and I have differing opinions on what constitutes toiletries. I wanna get some snacks, and I'd like to cook dinner for Steve as a thank you for hosting us like this. You can help me with that, by the way."

"Sounds good to me. I'd like to stop at a bookstore on the way, too. I recognize some of what I'm looking at out here." I gestured toward the entire natural world of the state of Florida. "But I feel at a loss by how much I don't know, so I'd like to get some field guides."

"Disconcerting to be off your range, eh?" Rosa asked. "Must be confounding to not know every plant you come across and all its medicinal and edible properties. Well, it'll give you something to do while we're stuck inside staying incognito."

"My thoughts exactly."

26

72 hours. Her target had been off the radar for almost 72 hours, now. The trip to the headwaters of Lake Chelan was a complete bust. The cabin hadn't been occupied in some time.

Marjory had planted a few more "spy eyes" at the places most frequented, including the bounty hunter's office. Not a god damned thing. Marjory never panicked, she only got angrier. But she was having more and more difficulty channeling her anger into productive action.

It was time to admit that MacKenzie Crow and his little chica had given her the slip.

The catch-22s with this job had screwed her, and she had to admit that most of them were of her own making. She'd have to see if Devil-Knight could pick them up somehow. Their phones were still in safety deposit lockup at a local bank. They weren't using any of the vehicles she'd bugged and tagged.

"I overplayed my hand."

In wanting to be seen as clever, and to put fear into her prey's heart, she'd gone too far. The bomb under the RAV had driven the rabbits into a hard-to-find hole, and once again, DevilKnight was her only hope. He not only was extremely good at the technical, but he was exceptional in finding new and inventive ways to locate people.

But he sure as hell didn't come cheap. This was going to be expensive.

"Hello, M." He said. "Did they slip away again?"

"How'd you know?" Marjory asked. "Scratch that. You always know. Yes. I had another interaction with them and the little bunnies ran into the weeds and hid. Their phones haven't moved. The relatives aren't contacting them. They could be anywhere. Fucking anywhere!"

"Didja ever watch that old movie, The Princess Bride?" He asked.

"I saw it once, several years ago when I was bored and there was nothing else worth watching. I found it dull."

"You remind me of something the Spaniard, Inigo Montoya said."

She rolled her eyes. "All right, you're dying to tell me, spit it out."

"He said, 'I have no head for strategy,' and so left the planning to the Dread Pirate Roberts. I'm your dread pirate."

So many replies she wanted to make, all of them unproductive. Marjory swallowed her pride, and said. "Then you think you can find them?"

"Sure. You know what concentric rings are? Like when you throw a pebble into a still pond?"

"Yes."

"In this modern age," he said, "only true experts such as myself can traverse the digital landscape without leaving traces. Unless they're camping out in the frozen pines, I'll find a hint of them. And when I do, I'll lead you right to them. Promise."

She believed him.

It was almost two days later before he contacted her again. DevilKnight called her on her secure phone, one provided by the Association, and gave her the good news.

"Found 'em, M!" he said, with the tone of a child who's about to surprise a parent with some new achievement. "Wanna know how?"

"Will knowing cost me extra?"

"Nope, the info on methodology is gratis. The results are not. I found a way to follow them through their pre-paid phones."

"Wait. I thought that was pretty much impossible."

"Maybe for most experts," he replied, condescension practically dripping from his tone, "I, however, am very well suited to thinking outside the box."

"For best results with your DevilKnight tracking tool, apply copious flattery at regular intervals," Marjory thought.

"There's no one better, Devil," she told him. "How on Earth did you ever find a way to hack pre-paids? I thought that burners didn't leave enough trail behind to track along, unless you knew the number of the phone?"

His excitement was tangible. Marjory doubted she could've stopped him telling her all about it. "It's the cell towers. Instead of trying to follow individual phones, I hacked into the cell tower nearest your guy's Uncle. I tapped into the transmission records for that tower and found what you normally find. Big company traffic, you know, like Verizon and T-Mobile for the most part. But on that tower, there was some pre-paid action. Guess how many prepaid phones were in the traffic?"

"Tell me."

"Precisely one. Some local calls, and a number of calls to a number in Florida. I went back through Gilbert Chambers' personal phone records and the number he called matches calls over the years to one Steven Hanger, who by the way has some heavily redacted military records. I recommend you involve him as little as possible in whatever you're planning. However, this man has a business, the details of *which I won't bore you, and the day before yesterday, he activated two phones for this business."*

If Marjory had been a bird dog, she would've gone on point. "You have my complete attention, Devil."

"I've been tracking the phones, to see if I could get a camera shot from something local. Sending a security camera photo to you right now. Are these two the ones you're looking for?"

A ping came from the iPad on the desk of the hotel room. Marjory picked it up and accessed her messages, accessing the untraceable faux account from DevilKnight. She saw the photo, labeled Robinson Nature Preserve, Bradenton Florida, and almost yelled for joy.

Two people were standing next to a Honda SUV. Compared to the other people in the background, they were as lean and muscular as greyhounds. They wore baseball caps and sunglasses, but she knew those exceptionally fit silhouettes at a glance.

"Devil, I'm starting to believe that you might be made out of magic. It's them!"

"I was sure it was," he replied. "I'm sending a secure PDF with the numbers to use to track their phone, and you'll note in the photo that we have the license plate of the car they're driving. I can program the Florida traffic system to give me updates whenever the CRV passes a traffic cam. My system will send you automatic updates every half hour. Between the phones and the license plate, your prey will be findable most of the time, M. Once again, the DevilKnight has triumphed. You may send the second half of your payment, and be assured that I am always able to help out my clients at the Association."

"The payment will be available in the next fifteen minutes, Devil," Marjory told him. She winced at just how much of her capital she'd be sending over. One thing that was drummed into her head was that you never, ever, screwed your assets, especially one who could report her to her higher ups.

"Then it's been a pleasure doing business, M. Hopefully you'll remember me on your next great adventure of conquest."

"Of course, DevilKnight. We all know there's no one better." she said, while silently imagining killing him before sending the money.

"I won't argue with you, M," he said. "My mama told me not to tell a lie."

27

After a light lunch at Taqueria El Güero taco wagon, Rosa and I went shopping at the local Walmart.

Having seen ourselves in the mirror before leaving Steve's, we'd both decided we looked a little too "modern day bounty hunter" and we needed a wardrobe change. I wanted to look a little less "end of the world survivor" and a little more "non-descript average Joe." In Florida, even in October, that meant shorts and T-shirts. Steve had suggested that we both buy rain jackets.

Rosa was glad to add to her airport purchases. She also bought herself a pastel peach-colored baseball cap to replace her black one, and a stylish pair of large-lensed sunglasses. She also picked out a pair of darker toned sunglasses for me too.

Rosa looked like the proverbial million bucks. When I was a kid, my mom let me read her Travis McGee novels, and the author described one of his female protagonists as the sort of woman who would look good even if dressed in a burlap sack. That described my girl perfectly.

As we walked back to the car, Rosa checked the weather

app on her phone. Looking at me she said; "It might be in our best interest to return to Fort Steve. The app says thunder with lightning in the afternoon. From what the sky to the north is telling me, I think it's right."

Driving to home base, I about dropped my jaw when we drove past the Smugglers Cove Alligator Mini Golf. Golfing with alligators? No doubt with a beer in hand.

I was running for my life, and it occurred to me this was not a pleasure tour. I kept having the sense the ball was about to drop. I should take my situation more seriously. But I couldn't help but smile: visiting an alien planet is fun.

Steve met us at the door, doing a quick scan of the surrounding houses as we came in the door. Several locks clicked as he shut the door behind us.

"Can't be too careful?" Rosa asked.

"While I doubt your problems from Washington State have followed you two down here, it pays to be watchful anyway. There've been a number of home invasions in the area lately, and all these locks ensure I have enough time to reach a hidden firearm." He gestured toward a cabinet near the entrance foyer. "Rosa, take a look behind that."

We looked into the space between the furniture and the wall. Half-covered by a nylon rifle scabbard, the stock of a tactical 12 gauge shotgun stood out the top of the nylon bag. A home invasion could be nipped in the bud pretty quickly with the double-aught buckshot shells I was sure were loaded in the weapon. It was a testament to how much Steve trusted us that we'd been taken into his confidence.

"If someone's kicking in the door," Rosa said. "I'm bee-lining for that scattergun."

"There are a number of other..." His sentence was interrupted by a roaring sound. "Looks like you two made it home just in time. Welcome to Florida in October."

I looked out through the screened-in porch. I could still

see the closer edge of the small lake, but the row of homes on the other side were completely obscured by a driving heavy rain. Water began cascading off of every surface, and I noted that the ends of Steve's gutter pipes ended in discrete plastic catchment barrels, hidden from the street by shrubs.

"Wow," I said. "Almost no transition. One moment just cloudy skies, the next moment you'd best hope you have a ticket for the Ark."

"Why do you think I advised you to get rain gear?"

"Steve," Rosa said. "You've been such a good host, I want to cook dinner tonight, if you have no objection."

"No objection whatsoever. You've seen what's in the cupboards. I tend to either live on canned food or going out to eat. A home-cooked meal? I'm all aboard for that. Though, that brings me to a certain subject."

"What's that?" I asked.

"Staying mobile, Mac. You and Rosa need to get on the road tomorrow. You two are going to be a lot safer if you're not staying in one place. I've written an itinerary for you both, along with phone numbers and websites of likely places to stay that won't require advance reservations. Nothing fancy, but decent places to stay 'far from the madding crowd.' Most of them near some outdoor attractions so you don't go stir crazy."

"It kinda sounds like you think we could be tracked here," Rosa said. "Lucas and Carmen didn't leave much of a trail to follow, thanks to Gilbert."

"It might seem unlikely," Steve replied, "but I've done work with some incredible intelligence-gathering people. The only sure way to not be tracked is to go completely analog, and even that isn't foolproof."

"We bow to your superior knowledge," I said. "We'll do some planning tonight and be on the road tomorrow morning."

———

That evening, Rosa made a most excellent dinner with my less than optimal help. It was a carne asada dish that she said was her Tia's recipe. It was delicious and there was very little left over after the three of us were done eating. Nothing left, actually.

The rain had disappeared as suddenly as it left, the weather near the coast being of a capricious nature. Steve, Rosa and I sat on the screened-in porch sipping beer.

"Another Cuervo, M'dear?" Steve asked Rosa.

"Please and thank you. Hey Steve, Can I ask you a question?"

"As long as it doesn't concern national security."

Rosa grinned at him. "What I wanted to ask is something that Mac and I have been curious about for some time. It's about Gilbert. You've known him for a long time, haven't you? And you're pretty close, right?"

Steve looked us both over with a speculative eye. "True. And your point?"

"Well, it's just that we're wondering how it is that he always seems to have enough money. We get a share of the bounty hunting profits, and while he and Vinnie get the majority shares, I know what the incoming checks are, and..."

"And you're curious where he gets the scratch to do some of the things he does, is that it?"

"We've asked, before," I said. "And quite frankly he treats us like mushrooms sometimes. You know, kept in the dark and fed..."

"I know what you mean, Mac. I was in the military."

"Well?" Rosa asked. "What *can* you tell us?"

"Not a darn thing. As far as you're concerned, anything concerning that subject is need to know, and..."

"And we don't need to know," I said.

"You got it."

"Can you tell us any stories about you and Gilbert?" Rosa asked. "I've been working for him for a number of years now, and frankly, neither Mac nor I know much about him outside of our personal experiences."

"He's the closest thing I have to a father," I said, "but I still hardly know much about his life. I know he was married, but I've never met his ex. I know he and you were in the wars, but he's never shared any of his experiences. Like I said, we're mushrooms."

"There are some experiences that you never share with your family, Mac. But I can tell you a funny story about me an' Gil."

"I'm all ears!"

"Me too," Rosa said, her expression now pensive. "Though I know what you mean about not sharing things about your service. I got some things that'll probably go to my grave with me from my time in the sandbox."

"Yeah, little sister," Steve reached over with his Heineken and clinked bottles with Rosa. "Anyway, on a different note, would you like to know how your uncle and I met Vinnie?"

"Heck yes," I said. "All I've ever gotten when I asked about him was that they served together."

"Okay. I really wouldn't call this a funny story, 'cause it's not, but I think you'll find it interesting. You'll forgive me if I don't go into too much detail. That might be frowned upon by certain people."

"Understood," Rosa said.

"It was the first time that Lieutenant Gil Chambers and I worked with a certain three-letter agency. I'm sure you can figure out which one. We were pretty good at getting in and out of hard situations, and that skill got us tapped for a mission with one of their agents."

"Which was?" I asked.

"A retrieval," Steve said, taking another swig of his Heineken. "One of their assets had signaled they were in danger of being found out and requested an extraction. Me, Gil and the spook were going into a "poorly controlled" area of the city to get this dude and escort him back to our base. All very covert."

"Seems pretty straightforward. Was this a night time OP?" Rosa asked.

"It was a night time OP, and it was anything but straight-forward," Steve paused a moment to collect his thoughts. "You see, our 'asset' turned out to be a double agent. He was feeding intel back to the militia he was a part of, while feeding the spooks crap in return. I guess his people decided an agent in the hand was worth a lot and had set up an ambush for us."

"Holy shit!" I said.

"Nothing holy about it, but it was definitely the shit. We get there and suddenly there are shooters trying to surround us. We were fortunate in two ways. One: they got overeager, sprung the trap before we were completely surrounded. Two: Gil and I, even though this little mission was supposed to be 'hush hush off the books,' had decided that our CO needed to know."

"Sounds like a good idea to me," Rosa said.

"Oh, believe me, it was," Steve said. "We'd managed to fight our way back to our Humvee, but the enemy had shot the hell out of the engine. All we could do was hunker behind the doors and keep shooting as long as we had ammo. Then they stopped firing."

"Why?" Rosa asked.

"Ah. Remember, they wanted the spook alive. They stopped shooting, and our 'asset' steps out from a building and begins negotiating. Tells Gil and I that if we leave the agent we can run away with our lives. First of all, that's not how the U.S. Military works, second neither Gil nor I thought for a moment that if we did run that we'd make it to the next block before they hunted us down and killed us."

"So, what'd you do?" I asked. Steve's story was building that 'need to know' thing that a good storyteller can stick in your brain.

"Remember we'd told our CO about this cluster ahead of time. The double agent is running his mouth one moment, and the next he just flops to the ground like a drunk passes out. Only he wasn't passed out. Half a second later, we heard the sound of a .50 caliber sniper rifle echo through the sky like Thor's thunder."

"Vinnie was a sniper," Rosa said.

"Yep," Steve grinned as he said it. "A damn good one. Our CO had positioned him and his spotter as overwatch. The enemy militia members, seeing their boy dead on the ground, decided to rush us. It was a mistake. Aside from Gil, me and the spook laying down fire from behind the Hummer, Vinnie was laying out our opponents at an alarming rate. We almost didn't need the fireteam that came up behind us and got us out of there."

"And that's how you met Vinnie?" Rosa asked.

"Actually, Gil and I sought him out later to buy him a beer. This was before the body building, and he was a skinny corporal with a deep Hawaii tan. He helped us out on more than one occasion after that. When Gil went into business, he offered me the partnership first, and when I wasn't interested in bounty hunting, he made Vinnie his partner. Don't think he's ever regretted that."

I sat back in my chair and took a sip of beer. I couldn't imagine how things would've gone if Steve had joined Uncle Gil. I liked Steve, but Vinnie was my big brother and I decided I was very happy with the way things had turned out.

28

The next morning, we left Steve's place with little fan-fare. Though we were immensely grateful to him for all his help, he wasn't the sort of man for sappy good-byes. In fact, he wasn't the sort for good-byes at all. Rosa and I had awoken early to find the house empty, with a note on the kitchen table.

"Mac and Rosa, I've gone out to run some errands. Make sure you lock the doors when you leave, and remember what we talked about. Stay as old school as you can. Pay cash if possible. Use the phones only as needed, move on every two nights. These strategies will make you very hard to keep up with even if someone is on to you. Safe travels, ——Steve. PS: Destroy this note when you leave, can't be too careful."

"No lengthy farewells in this household," Rosa said.

"Some people don't handle goodbyes well," I replied. "Or maybe he would like us and our troubles to just move on down the road."

"Let's just assume the former, Mac. We ready to get on the road?"

"Everything is loaded in the car. I think we're ready to go, unless you can think of something else we need to buy."

"Actually, there is. Steve's comment about being prepared got me thinking. We are down here with our butts hanging in the wind. To be honest with you, after everything he's told us, I think we should arm ourselves."

She wasn't wrong, though I'd thought we could just play tourist while we were down here, not contemplating shooting anyone. Steve's paranoia was contagious, though. Even packing our stuff in the car I'd kept my head on a swivel, trying to see trouble if it should happen to be coming.

Thing was, if trouble came, Rosa and I would have to take it on with knives, fists and feet. That sort of thing, in this modern era where guns were more numerous than people to carry them, was not a particularly good strategy. No one survives taking a knife to a gunfight.

"I'm not up on the laws for gun purchase in Florida," I said. "Can we even get one here without a ton of paperwork?"

"This is Florida. The 'stand your ground' state. If you were looking for a place to find a gun without much regulation, this is the state to do it. Also, I talked to Steve last night, and he knows a shop that'll supply us and ignore the three-day waiting period."

"Okay, if you think we might need 'em, let's go shopping."

29

What to do, what to do.

Florida. Literally the farthest from where she was in the conti-nental United States, and of course those two little shits had bugged out there.

Or had they?

Marjory was coming to realize that these people weren't as unaware as she'd thought. They were cagey and leaving a false trail was just the sort of thing they'd do. All the while still hiding out here.

It wouldn't be that hard to have a ringer go to Florida, as unlikely as it seemed. Chambers seemed to be a lot more knowledge-able than a civilian should be, and she cursed herself for not digging into the history of the family members more. It hadn't seemed like a priority, them being based out here in podunk-land.

Could it be possible this was a ruse that had fooled even Devil-Knight? Or was it just as he said, just as it seemed.

No. She'd seen the photo of them. They had to be there.

God. Marjory wished she'd just put a bullet into young MacKenzie when she had the chance. If she left, using up more of her rapidly dwindling funds, she'd have no fallback cash. DevilKnight's services hadn't come cheap. Not remotely cheap.

And if the whole thing went south, Marjory had no intention of waiting around for the organization to sanction her. The fact that they'd frozen her main account with their bank indicated to her that they weren't about to let her go, bygones being bygones.

No, if they weren't going to take her back, she'd need every resource to go on the run.

If she flew to Florida now, and it was somehow a damn ruse, maybe with look-a-likes, who knew?

She might not be afforded the time to finish the contract at all. The Association wasn't giving her unlimited time to prove herself.

If only she could be in two places at once.

The idea sprang into her brain full-blown and, her brow furrowed, she wrestled with it. If the association ever found out...

But it could work.

30

Rosa and I were on our own.

We'd had a support system for most of the escape from our home turf, Uncle Gil on one end, Steve on the other. Now, we would make our own decisions and our own mistakes. Hopefully non-fatal ones.

Steve's itinerary had been a 'suggestion' and if we felt it necessary, we would not only go off the plan, we'd become invisible to it. Invisible as long as all our safeguards had worked. For the time being though, we'd stick to the plan religiously.

Our first stop once we were on the road, was to stop at a gun shop. I realize that there are those who would object to this strenuously, but the honest truth of the matter was that someone had threatened to kill me and possibly Rosa too, as collateral damage. Under such circumstances, only a fool would believe they could preserve their lives with love, peace and kindness alone.

We stopped at the place Steve had recommended, *Walt's Old Time Hardware,* on the outskirts of the town of Oldsmar. *Walt's* was the very definition of a hole in the wall business, a tiny old building on a sandy lot surrounded by more modern buildings. When we walked in, the front half of the place was indeed a small ACE hardware, with a few customers wandering the aisles. A petite older lady wearing a red 'hardware store' apron sat on a stool behind the cash register. Her hair was dyed an astonishing shade of copper red, and though she was smiling, I just got a vibe of 'mind your manners' from her. To one side of the counter there was a door with a heavy metal lattice cover.

"Excuse me, M'am," Rose stepped forward.

"You can call me Ophelia, Miss," she said, pointing to her nameplate. "How can I help you?"

"Ok, Ophelia, we're looking for the 'other' business," Rosa said under her breath, quietly but unapologetically. Rosa had a way of taking command.

"You young people lookin' to get heeled, are you?" she asked, her accent soft, cultured sounding. "I'm sorry, Darlin's, but we only sell to a small clientele, mostly by referral. Don't want to be sellin' to the wrong folks, you understand. Not that I'm sayin' y'all are those types, but we got to be careful."

"Um...what would be the wrong types you mean, Ma'am?" I asked.

"Bangers. Tweakers. General hoodlums. We don't care about race, creed or religion, but Earl don't want none of our guns used for crimes."

"Earl?" Rosa asked. "What happened to Walt?"

The lady laughed a bright, musical laugh that I couldn't help but smile along with. "Oh Honey, no one named Walt has been here for... must be close to forty years now. Earl bought the place from the previous owner and was disinclined to change the name, you know, for business reasons."

"Ah, sure," Rosa said. "We were referred to you by a gentleman named Steve Hanger. He said you'd know him and that he vetted us. I have his business card with me, if you want to call and verify with him."

She looked us over for a full minute without replying. Then she said: "Y'know what? I've got a good feeling about you two. You just don't seem like hard cases to me. Let me buzz you in to see Earl."

"I dunno, Ma'am," I said, faking trying to be sneaky and pointing at Rosa behind my hand, "she's pretty dang tough. Me, not so much."

"Oh mah goodness. A young man willing to admit that a woman might be more knowledgeable than he is. Truly it is a new age." She smiled and hit a button behind the counter. The latticed door opened and she ushered us in.

We walked into a much smaller space, whose every bit of wall space had a firearm hanging from it. There were so many, that sections of the wall resembled the old game Tetris in the way they were layered in. Behind the counter was a small gnome of a man who appeared to be around a hundred and fifty years old. He smiled at us with a mouth full of exceptionally white teeth that could only be dentures at his age, and gestured for us to come in.

"Come in! Come in, young folks," he said. Just now I didn't feel that young, but I supposed anyone under eighty was young to him.

"Hello, sir," I bowed my head slightly.

He smiled at the polite greeting. "You can call me Earl. And who is this young lady?"

"Carmen," she replied, offering her hand, which he seemed to appreciate.

"So, your mother was a fan of Bizet, was she?"

Rosa looked a bit nonplused.

"Georges Bizet. Whose most famous opera was 'Carmen', about a femme fatale who bewitched men."

"He had that right." I smiled.

"And led them to their deaths," Earl added.

Rosa smiled nervously, which wasn't her usual look.

"I guess if Ophelia has buzzed you in, that you must be in the market for a weapon of some sort. How can I help? Do you need something for hunting? Home defense? Everyday carry? I have to tell you now, if you're looking for 'army men' guns, you came to the wrong place."

"We kind of figured that, from the look of things," Rosa replied, regaining her composure.

I looked around to see what Rosa already noticed and I missed. Being on high alert for the apex predator, I had my eyes on all the other people in the store.

And then I saw it: it wasn't what was there but what *wasn't* there.

Every other firearms seller that I've ever frequented had multiple variations of the AR-15 platform covering the walls. Ofttimes, that particular weapon took up over half the selling space. Not so here. Every weapon on the wall had a civilian look to them, though I noted that some fired the same .223 Remington round just as efficiently as the more military looking weapons.

"Um... we are here for some personal protection," Rosa told him. "We're concerned about being attacked. We're both used to Glocks, if you have those."

"Every kind they sell, Miss Carmen." Earl walked us over to a section of wall, that in a less compacted sales space we might've noticed on our own. Forest for the trees. "Plus ammunition, accessories, whatever you need." He gave us a sidelong look. "You needing protection from something... someone specific? Or you just want to make sure you're covered, just in case?"

I was hesitant to discuss our situation with strangers, even one as kindly-seeming as this old man, so it was a surprise to me when Rosa answered him.

"We've been... threatened," she said. "We're from out of state, and we *think* we won't be bothered here, but we can't be sure."

"Sounds like you might be on the run?"

"Not from the law, sir. From someone... shall we say... you wouldn't want to sell to. We came to Florida to get away from that person. But we can't be sure we got away clean. Thus, we feel we want protection."

"Seems prudent," he replied.

———

We were well equipped when we left. In addition to two Glock pistols, Rosa had also purchased a back-up weapon, a small compact 9mm, as well as ammunition, spare mags and a small under-the-seat gun safe. There were places, even in Florida, where firearms just wouldn't be allowed so we needed to be able to secure and conceal the guns in the SUV.

We'd both bought close fitting small-of-the-back holsters. With untucked shirts, it would take close inspection to notice we were packing, but we didn't want to invite trouble by taking the Glocks somewhere we could get arrested for carrying.

It is unfortunate that such measures were necessary. I'd certainly be happy to never have to draw down on another human being again for the rest of my life, much less pull a trigger on them. But even the most ardent pacifist has to admit that the most dangerous creatures we face aren't grizzlies, crocodiles, tigers or bears. The most lethal threat to peaceful people, since the time of the stone age, has always been other humans.

In modern America, the number of deaths by say... bears, is infinitesimally small compared to the number of people murdered by others of their own species. The people who are willing to attack other people don't care about ideals or morals, just brutal efficiency.

We left Oldsmar, heading west toward Dunedin, then north on U.S. 19. Traffic was heavy heading out, though it started to thin the farther out from the Tampa area we drove.

"Wow, billboard much?" Rosa said, looking out the passenger window at the steady stream of huge advertising placards along the highway. "You don't see this back home."

"The legislature in Washington State banned billboards on highways decades ago," I said. "The only place you'll see much of that sort of thing is within actual city limits. I think that also was about the same time when most community service sentences for misdemeanors became litter pickup along the roads up there. Of course, we don't have cool palm trees in the Northwest."

"Looks like about eighty percent of the billboards are for ambulance chasers." She noted. "Remind me not to get in a fender bender down here."

"Or to be based out of Camp LeJeune." I noted.

"Hey, Mac. There were several people out on a yacht, and one of them was a lawyer." I raised an eyebrow at Rosa, sensing a bad joke coming.

"Yeah?"

"They were throwing food trash over the side, and several sharks were following the boat. A big wave hit, and the lawyer fell overboard, right in the midst of the sharks. Know what happened?"

"I assume there was one less lawyer." I said.

"Nope. The sharks actually lifted him up and he climbed back aboard the yacht."

"What? Why?"

"Professional courtesy."

31

Wade Tyler didn't have a bad life.

Do a job here, a job there, not having to work a day otherwise, long as he was careful with his cash. And he was definitely making a reputation for himself. Still, there was more than a little risk, and he surely thought he should be paid <u>better</u>.

Needless to say, he was thrilled when the person who'd introduced him to his current trade called.

"Mavis!" he said, not quite able to keep the excitement from his voice. "Tell me you're here in the Sunshine state."

"Afraid not, M'dear," the sultry voice purred. "I am as far away from Florida as you can get in the lower 48. How y'all doin' there, Wade? Use any of the skills I taught you?"

"Henh. Just the professional ones. My business, shall we say, has greatly increased thanks to all your tips. Still not makin' the big money yet, but I don't need to work construction no more." He said. "So, I can tell you about what I been doin'; maybe you'll consider taking me on as your official apprentice like you hinted about."

"Oh Wade, Darlin,' you are still in the larval state. Someday down the line, I'll come down there and give you some serious training. But you're young, give it a little time."

"Maybe when you get down here we can take up where we left off on... other activities too?" Wade's heartbeat sped up at the mere thought of what they'd done during their 'private time' in the motel.

Her chuckle made his heart race even more. "Oh Wade, that would be fun wouldn't it? But sadly, or maybe not sadly, this is a business call."

"Seriously?"

"As a heart attack, handsome. As part of your journey along the path, I have a personal contract I want you to take on. Just between you and me. The quarry is small-time, so I can only pay you twenty thousand. You in?"

Twenty grand? That was five times what he'd been getting. It made him realize just how low on the totem pole he actually was, but that much for one quick hit was big-time money.

"Yeah," he said. "I think I can do it for that, 'specially since it's you. I consider it part of my training. I'm totally in."

"Excellent," she purred. "I'll be sending photos, license plates, and general info to you on your business phone. You did get a pre-paid for your business phone like I told you, didn't you?"

"You bet. How'm I gonna find 'em though? You know where they're stayin'?"

"I'm tracking them electronically. You'll be getting updates from me, though they'll be sent through different phone numbers each time. Little tip for you, Wade, if you're not already doin' it, never hang onto a dirty phone too long. Have a phone where clients can contact you, and when they do, immediately give them a burner number to call and hang up. Incriminating phones need to be trashed often."

"Oh yeah, definitely only hangin' on to the biz phone for a short time," Wade said, cringing inside. He'd been using the same burner for a year now, and doing all his business on it.

"Good. I'll get you close to them, you do the job," she told him. "Clean and quick, nothing fancy, just bullets where they should be or a bomb if you have to. Understand? Don't embellish."

"Can do. I won't let you down."

"I know you won't, sweetie. I knew there was special potential in you as soon as we struck up a conversation last year. Now give me your business number, and I'll send you what you need to know."

––––––––

Well, it was done. She's made the plunge and hired a subcontractor. Even with Devilknight's help, she was worried that MacKenzie Crow and Rosa Fernandez might somehow escape if they weren't dealt with immediately.

And if the Association ever found out what she'd done, she was dead.

If Wade could actually pull this off, with the little training he had, she'd get on a fast, cheap flight to Florida, so she could claim the final kill. She'd start looking for a ticket now.

Wade, of course, would need to die once the hit was done. Timothy and the others must never know what she'd done. If Wade was successful, her path was set. He had good instincts, and she'd given him good basic training. If he flubbed it, she'd have to make the choice between flying down and trying to salvage things or making a run for it.

Too bad about Wade, though. When they'd met, she'd been lonely and bored. Maybe a little under the influence of certain relaxing substances too. He'd obliquely bragged about being a hard case and she hadn't been able to resist showing him what a real hard case was.

Marjory had impressed him alright, in more ways than one. She'd also told him more about herself than was prudent, but now she was glad she hadn't decided to kill him then. If he could get the job done, he'd be the perfect throw-away tool.

This was probably a very bad idea, but when you were desperate, you had to take chances. In the meantime, maybe it'd be a good idea to find a remote cabin for rent, maybe on one of the islands off of British Columbia.

Someplace completely off the grid.

Just in case.

32

Venice is breathtaking at this time of day.

The best view of the Floating City with its ancient waterways, Renaissance architecture, and charming bridges was in St. Mark's Square at sunset, watching the light cast golden mosaics onto St. Mark's Basilica as another glorious day came to a close.

Unfortunately, the unwanted task assigned to him had robbed Timothy of the pleasure he ordinarily felt at this scene.

Vanessa had called.

When the head of the Association calls and tells you, "I need to see you. Here. As soon as you can catch a flight," things were going to be tense. This wasn't a meeting of the primes, this was him being called onto the carpet.

And he damn well knew why too. Marjory had no idea that the Association-provided equipment she was using allowed them to monitor her communications. Since Timothy had interceded for her, he'd been tasked with keeping track of what she was doing, and none of it was impressive. Quite the opposite.

And he'd had to forward that information on. That's why he'd been summoned.

He'd put so much effort into training that woman, and now she was dragging him down with her. This is what happens when you let a moment of sentiment and wishful thinking keep you from making the hard call early on.

Walking purposefully, Timothy entered the Palazzo Benito on the Grand Canal. The building was old and grand and unlike some of the surrounding antiquities, it had been updated with the most advanced surveillance technology available. The uniformed door man quietly held the door open for him.

Inside, various pieces of art were displayed and tourists milled about viewing them. Timothy traversed the huge lobby and moved into a back corridor. There, an Armani-suited security man quietly asked him if he was armed.

"Seriously?" Timothy asked. "Isn't everyone here?"

"I'll need you to divest yourself in the next room, sir," was the reply. "Then step through the scanner. Once you're cleared, you can take the elevator up."

Timothy did so. Once cleared to proceed by a cold-eyed young woman, also in a fine suit (Gucci if he wasn't mistaken, and he wasn't), he began the trip upward to learn his fate.

Disarming him hadn't just been about security. It'd also been instruction in how vulnerable he was, his many skills at violence be damned. He exited the elevator into a spacious office, adorned with several pieces of art that he was fairly sure were supposed to be in museums. It was unlikely that this office displayed copies.

A young woman, seated at a desk gave him a reflexive dazzling smile and told him, "She'll see you now. You can go right in."

"Thank you," he said, and opened the heavy oaken door. At the end of a stupidly expensive carpet, a very ornate desk sat. Behind it, much more austere and business-like, sat the head of the Association.

"Hello, Vanessa. You're looking lovely, as always."

"Thank you for noticing, Timothy. I do work at it," she replied. Vanessa was in her early fifties, and the business attire and jewelry she wore could have financed a fine automobile. Her makeup was flawless and only accentuated her luminous brown eyes. But Vanessa *was a business woman and flattery wouldn't go far. "But, let's, as the Americans say, 'cut to the chase,' shall we?"*

Usually there was banter. The lack thereof informed him of just how nervous Marjory had made his peers. "You've read my reports."

"You wouldn't be here in person if I hadn't. Oh Timothy, this is a very unfortunate turn of events. This apprentice you convinced us to give another chance is turning into a train wreck. The ill-advised terror campaign, the using of association resources without permission, and now...." Vanessa shook her head in disbelief.

"And now," Timothy finished for her, "she's contacted an outsider to do the work for her. I know. I am as astonished as you, Vanessa, and more than a little horrified with her actions."

"Oh, my dear Timothy, the horror is not over. There's something I'm sure you don't know. Your Marjory, like most of us, avails herself of the exceptional medical services provided by the Association. After I read your report, I did a deep dive on everything Marjory. Doing so, I found something that'd been hidden in her last visit to her doctor. She's using."

All he could do was stare. For the first time in his life, Timothy was speechless. "I assume you mean beyond light recreational use?"

"I think we've all experienced a few mood changers, Timothy. What was in the report, was a drug that is addictive. The level in her bloodstream was indicative of usage far beyond merely recreational," Vanessa said. "I can tell from your expression that this is news to you."

"I... Yes. Yes it is."

"The doctor, who should have red-flagged this, I assure you, has been disciplined. The report is over a year old, and perhaps explains the clusterfuck that her last assignment turned into. She may not be a total addict, but as you can see..."

"Oh Christ, Vanessa. If I'd known this, I swear to you I would've slipped something fatal into her drink when last we met," he said. "I just put so much work into training that woman."

"I understand that, Timothy. I'm sure by now that we both see her as unsalvageable and a menace to our Association. This is, in the end,

your screw up. You know how the Board feels about screw ups, particularly ones threatening our invisibility."

"Of course."

I would suggest that you clean up your mess as quickly as possible," Vanessa added, "lest you be painted with the same brush as your Marjory."

"I will end this... I will end her, as soon as I can get there. I'll be on a plane tonight, and I will take care of this. The Association will not have to worry about any exposure. I will make her disappear."

"Good. Then I think we are done here." She turned those stunning eyes up to his. "Timothy. I feel the need to warn you that your apprentice has put you on very shaky ground with the Association. Very. Shaky. Ground. As an old friend, I thought you should know."

"I see. Thank you, Vanessa. I'll see myself out."

He closed the heavy door behind him and entered the elevator. It was all he could do to not shiver. He'd do as he said, but it was possible it was time to go Ghost Protocol.

33

If you're not using GPS, it wouldn't be that hard to drive through the town of Homosassa, Florida and not realize it. From the occasional business on the side of the road to suddenly being in 'civilization' was a very quick transition.

Once again, Rosa and I were grateful for the new pre-paid phones Steve had lent us. Without GPS, we could've blown on through before realizing we were at our next destination. It wasn't that it was a super small town, it was just spread out.

A bit of backtracking down various side roads, and we came to our hideout for the next couple of nights. It was an older canal home, not new and shiny but well-kept, sitting on one of the many side canals in the area. This was damp country, and the driveway had moss growing along its sides. The backyard had spots where the owners were losing a battle with palmetto plants. A small deck sat over the canal in the back yard. It was a pretty place, especially in the warm Florida fall. Spanish moss grew from the trees and swayed in the breeze.

"Wonder what this place is like in July," I said.

"I'd guess hot, humid and 'squitoey. I mean with this

much slow-moving water, there'd have to be mosquitoes, right?" Rosa replied.

"Unless they've got some good mosquito control programs. Look at all the fish in the canal." As I said it, a large, oddly-finned fish went jumping past us and on down the canal in a series of leaps. Below me, I could see sunfish and perch in profusion.

You could probably have fish for dinner every night if you knew how to run a rod. Back home, the only fish this easy to see would be carp in the shallows.

"Mac, check these out." I turned to see Rosa pointing at a pair of lime green plastic kayaks. "I've never been in one of these before. You think we could try 'em out before we move on?"

"I don't see why not," I said, checking an app on one of the phones. "Weather app says that it'll be sunny tomorrow. Let's take a run in them tomorrow after the sun's been up for a while."

I'm not quite sure when we transitioned from being on the run to being on vacation, but I realized that my shoulders had relaxed and for a while I could breathe easy.

Rosa and I unloaded the car, except for our original bug-out bags, and then drove into town to find a grocery store. We picked up a few things for the fridge and went back to our new home as it started to get dark.

That night was the first time in a month that Rosa and I had felt relaxed enough to do more than sleep when we went to bed that night.

———

The next day, we played tourist. You might think that it would've been better to stay indoors, hiding out the entire time, but our way of thinking was that if anyone was tracking us, being in one spot was a sure way to get found and attacked.

After a snack-ish breakfast on the back canal deck, Rosa and I tried out the canals in the lime-green kayaks. After a morning of floating along quiet waters, watching the local but exotic-to-us birds and fish, being passed only by motor boats creeping along at barely more than an idle, we both decided that kayaks were in our future back home.

"Nice of the boaters to go along so slow through here," I said. "Must be to keep peaceful relations with the people that live along the canals."

"Actually, I think it might be for the benefit of these guys here," Rosa said, pointing to a large fat cigar shape floating next to us.

"Is that what I think it is?" I asked, my heart skipping a beat.

"If you think it's a manatee," Rosa said. "Look! There's another one."

The slow-moving creature swam under my kayak. It surfaced for a moment, took a breath and then took a look at me. My Florida experience took a big turn upward at that moment, as this curious, gentle being and I shared a moment in the stream of time. We sat and watched them feed for a good while before they moved on into the main river.

You see videos of the other creatures on this tiny planet of ours, but you don't really have a true connection with them until you're looking into each other's eyes. My abilities in the woods have gifted me with this feeling on more than one occasion, though the grizzly in the Canadian Rockies hadn't been the warmest feeling of my life.

I noticed though, that both of the manatees had nicks and what looked like old cuts on their backs. Evidently not everyone was careful with their boats.

———

We finished out the day with a visit to Homosassa state park, containing an amazing deep-water spring and a zoo. The spring was astonishing, putting out thousands of gallons per minute and surrounded by a carousel of large fish endlessly circling the source.

The zoo affected me the same as almost all of them do. The animals looked bored and unhappy, which didn't do much for my own mood. Rosa seemed to be fascinated though, so I locked my jaw shut on the acidic comments crying to escape my mouth. Seeing our first alligators of the trip simply made me want to be very careful anytime I was going to be near water while we were here.

Later that evening we had an unexpected dining experience. At the riverside restaurant where we were enjoying a meal of fried seafood, the manager came along and handed us each a U.S. flag.

"Um.. " I said. "What's this for?" The flag was nice, and I didn't really think he was gifting them to us.

"It's Tuesday," he said. "You come on Tuesday, you get to be part of the ceremony. If you're new, just watch, you'll see."

I had the feeling that the ceremony, whatever it was, wasn't optional.

A few moments later, the song 'Proud to be an American' began to play over the speakers and the patrons around me began waving their small flags with gusto. Then the manager made a speech about service people and the sacrifices they made for an indifferent public. He also pointed to the door and said anyone who didn't agree was welcome to leave. The door he pointed to was the one with the plank over the river.

I looked over at Rosa. Her eyes were sparkling with the traces of tears, and I felt guilty that the whole affair hadn't affected me like it did her.

After it was over, I sounded her out about it.

"That was really something, wasn't it?"

"Yeah," she said, wiping her eye with a knuckle. "I think that would've affected anyone who'd served. Probably seemed a bit cheesy to you, eh Mac?"

"I don't think I understood it like you do, sweetie."

"That's not surprising. No offense, Mac, but if you haven't served, you can't understand how a little recognition feels. Vets get politicians who say 'Thank you for your service,' and then make huge cuts to the V.A. Or use the military as a political football. A lot of civilians say the same thing with no idea what was sacrificed in their name. Friends lost. Limbs lost. Souls lost."

"I'm... I'm sorry."

"It's not your fault. If you weren't there, you can't know." She took a deep breath. "Hey. Let's settle up and get out of here, okay? I think I'm ready to go. Where are we going to land tomorrow?"

"We'll leave Homosassa early tomorrow and head north. We'll end up at a place called Cedar Key. Rumor has it that John Muir stayed there while recovering from malaria."

"Well. Can't miss that, can we?"

34

Traffic. The fucking traffic.

Starting out from his tiny bungalow in Key Largo a little later in the afternoon than he'd planned, Wade had hit every major traffic snarl that the Florida interstate system could throw at him. Huge rush hour constipations. Car wrecks with lookyloos slowing down by the hundreds to gawk, tourists in big RV's that had no idea where they were going or what they were doing.

The only thing that kept him from blowing his stack was the need to stay low-profile. In the time that he'd spent with Mavis, he'd never seen her get emotional, not even for a moment. That was how professionals acted. That thought calmed him and helped him keep his frustration under control. He used the deep-breathing techniques his mentor had shown him to dial it down.

Things like being stuck in traffic would've blown his gaskets before. Now, he no longer beat on his horn, though the more egregious nitwits among his fellow motorists still made him take deep breaths to get his irritation and desire to put a dozen holes in them under control.

No one's perfect.

By the time he'd gotten far enough north to be past the worst of it, the sun was long gone, and he had a new problem. The narrow state route he was on had only a few motes of civilization in a sea of forest and swamp. But it did have wildlife. Lots of wildlife that liked to wander up on the road at inopportune moments.

He found himself dodging possums, skunks (definitely didn't want to hit them) deer and in one instance, he barely missed a large alligator. If his Jeep hadn't had the bright halogens, he probably would've had big bloody dents all over.

It was the middle of the night when he saw the all-night diner along the roadway, and his stomach reminded him that he hadn't eaten since noon. It was damn close to midnight now. You didn't want to be starving when you killed people. He didn't like to kill on an empty stomach. He thought about being hungry the entire time, and not focusing on the job. He pulled over.

The food, flavor-enhanced as it was by hunger, caused its own problem though: he had been so excited the previous night that he hadn't gotten much sleep. The heavy meal hadn't done much for his alertness. A few miles further on, and he had to yank the wheel of the car hard to keep from driving off into the ditch when he went into a semi-doze.

He pulled over and off to the side in the driveway of a local self-storage company, the various lights from the enclosure providing illumination as he adjusted his chair to the most comfortable position he could manage under the circumstances. A rolled-up sweatshirt formed a pillow and he quickly drifted off.

———

"Hey buddy. Mister! Wake up!"

Wade looked up groggily, and a shooting pain went through his neck. It was light out, and a large pear-shaped man was tapping on his window.

"You can't park here, man. This ain't a rest stop."

Wade checked to make sure that the bag with his weapons was

closed. He turned the key enough to roll down his heavily-tinted side window. "It was either park here or go off the road last night. Didn't mean to cause y'all any difficulties."

Wade had an urge to show this asshole who he really was, but that wasn't the way of the professional. Quiet and friendly kept you off the radar much better than truthful and angry.

"I hear you, man. But it's nine a.m., the facility is opening up, and I need you to move along, okay?"

Wade started the car. "Sure. Sorry for the trouble. I'm headin' west. Is there a coffee shop along the way here anytime soon? I could really use a jolt of caffeine."

"'Bout four miles down the road. There's a little coffee stand, y'know, one of those trailer ones, and the girls they hire there are all cute little high-school girls. The tip jar there is always full."

"Great, thanks."

He'd just pulled out on the highway when his business phone pinged. Glancing at the screen, he pulled over. It was from Mavis.

"Why aren't you in Homosassa? You've been in the same spot for hours," her text read.

Well damn. Looks like the marks weren't the only ones Mavis was tracking.

"I was delayed going north. Finally had to pull over and get a few Z's," he replied. "I'm on the way now. I'll be in Homosassa..." he checked the time in the corner of the screen, "..about two hours from now. They won't get away; I'll just need to wait until they're somewhere private."

"They've already gotten away," she texted back. "My tracking says they've gone back to the highway and are heading north. My gut says they're moving every couple of days, which doesn't make your job any easier."

"I'll get on my way then, maybe I can catch them."

"Just get to Homosassa and start north. Their pattern says they'll find a place to stay and go to ground for a few days. I'll let you know when I've got their next stop pin-pointed. We can strategize after that."

"I'm on my way," Wade told her. "I'll check in at Homosassa, and you can tell me if the plan changes."

"I'll keep you up to date. And nap on your own time from now on. Get the job done. You can sleep when you're dead."

Wade didn't quite know what to make of that last, hopefully a figure of speech, sentence.

35

The drive to Cedar Key was uneventful. The palms and palmetto along the highway, so exotic at first, had faded into the background. We were well out of anything remotely urban and had the wide highway mostly to ourselves. Rosa was driving while I looked at the scenery, but the flat landscape was starting to get a bit monotonous.

I spent part of my time perusing a Florida state atlas I'd picked up at a gas station. The thick book had every side road, highway and interstate in the entire area of Florida. I, however, was using it to find state parks, nature preserves and anything that would allow Rosa and I to explore without staying in areas likely littered with cameras.

Besides, if you're going to Florida, the main attractions should be outdoors.

"There's a spot here called Cedar Key Scrub State preserve," I said. "And also, near our cabin is the Lower Suwannee National Wildlife preserve."

"Sounds good, Mac," Rosa replied. "But I may just want to sit on a deck at a restaurant, eat food and sip beer. Maybe we can do that tomorrow."

"Maybe we can scope the area out for a run tomorrow too," I replied. "I haven't put on my runners since Bradenton. I'm gonna get soft."

"Our cabin is outside Cedar Key. Maybe there'll be some good surfaces alongside the road into town that we can run on."

"We can hope."

We were on the long cut-off road to our next lodgings when Rosa pulled over. "Mac, check your bars. How's our connection here?"

"It's... wow. Four bars." I looked around. and in the distance, not too far from the road, I saw a tower against the hazy mid-morning sky.

"Since we're nowhere near where we're going to stay. How about we use this opportunity to get in touch with Steve? I'd like to know if Gil's had any luck tracking down our stalker."

"If nothing else, Steve can pass on that we're still alive."

Rosa took out her pre-paid iPhone and dialed Steve's number.

"Hey. It's Carmen," she said when he picked up. "Just checking in. Lucas and I are doing fine and sticking to the plan. Just wanted to get an update on how things are at home, and if any progress on our problem has happened." She nodded as she listened. "Uh-huh. I see. Thanks Steve. I won't tell you our location, but so far, we haven't seen any indication that anyone is after us here. I better keep this brief, though. We'll make contact in a few days. Bye."

"What's happening at home?" I asked.

Rosa took a second to gather her thoughts. "They haven't made any progress on finding your stalker. Evidently our uni-bomber hasn't made contact in any way since we left, which kinda worries me."

"How so?"

"Look, Mac. What that says to me, is that our opponent

knows we're out of the area. Gil was assuming they'd make more efforts, thinking we'd still be there, but there's been nothing. If they knew we were gone that fast, somehow we might be compromised. It just makes me want to grow eyes in the back of my head."

We both sat in the afternoon sun, furiously trying to think of any way that the assassin could've tracked us to Florida. "Rosa, I still, for the life of me, can't think of any way that we've screwed up. They may know we're gone, but that doesn't mean that they know *where* we've gone."

"Maybe not," she replied. "But I was starting to relax a bit. Now, I feel like I'd better ratchet the ol' situational awareness back up."

"We should definitely keep our eyes open, but let's not devolve in to mass paranoia. We can't be so hyper-vigilant that it becomes exhausting. We let that happen, and our awareness is going to tank anyway."

"You're right," she said. "Let's just remember that we can't let our guard all the way down until this is over."

———

Cedar Key was a sleepy little place, beloved by the few tourists who went there—not a lot of activity—which suited our purposes to a "T". I was pretty stoked because we managed to get the Firefly Resort cabin where John Muir wrote, *A Thousand Mile Walk to the Gulf.*

I knew I wasn't on vacation; I was running from a killer. But I don't have that many heroes in life, so I was interested to share the same space and energy. Muir was not in Cedar Key under the best of circumstances either—he was forced to stop and recover from malaria.

Maybe I would learn something about survival here.

Muir arrived in Cedar Key seven weeks after setting out from Indiana. While recovering from malaria in Cedar Key, he wrote the recounting of his long walk, including glimpses of life in the post-Civil War South.

It was here in Cedar Key that Muir first expressed his belief that nature was valuable for its own sake, not merely because nature was useful for man. This principle guided John Muir throughout his life. In early 1868, he left Cedar Key and eventually settled in California, where he helped establish the Yosemite National Park.

My kind of guy.

Once we'd checked into our cabin, which overlooked a tidal bay filled with birds and clams, we decided that we wanted to eat. We put our gear, except the bug-out bags, into the room and drove into the town proper. Rosa got her deck view, meal and a beer at a local restaurant.

A part of me wished that we hadn't called Steve. *Steamers* waterfront restaurant was crowded, and we'd only gotten the deck as a stroke of luck and had to wait ten minutes for someone to come along and clear off the previous occupant's dishes. Neither of us minded that, as the view out toward the ocean was wonderful.

The drawback was that there was a huge picture window behind us that we had to sit with our backs to. The likelihood that a killer would have the balls to shoot us in a crowded restaurant, through the window, was very low, but never impossible.

The assassin hadn't just threatened our lives, they'd stolen our harmony. Yeah, I know that seems like a "well, duh" revelation, but having it in the forefront of our minds seemed to make it sting even more.

We walked along the small waterfront area, drifting in and out of tourist shops, not wanting to clutter our situation with trinkets, but needing to do something to pass the time. Unlike in Homosassa, I found myself on constant alert, trying to see anyone that might be taking interest in or following us.

No one there; just other tourists.

We both knew we couldn't keep this up forever.

36

Wade drove into Cedar Key that evening. Mavis had unerringly guided him along the target's trail, even giving him the name of the smallish resort they were staying at.

There was just one problem. She couldn't pin-point which one of the fifteen or so cabins they were staying in. The entire place was inside of a large six-foot board fence. Mavis' maps simply didn't provide that level of detail.

Switching to Google Earth hadn't done the job either. Nor could she link into a current satellite image due to the heavy tree cover inside the fence.

There was no way he could sneak inside and look through fifteen cabins full of sleeping people. Nor could he find the quarry by their car, because it was out here, outside the fence parked in a small lot along a busy street.

"To be this close and not be able to finish the job is so gawdamn frustrating!"

All Wade could do was sit in his car in the dark and try not to do something that would compromise the mission. Several plans went through his mind, each more over the top than the last, even burning the place down. But assassination was a precision art. There was no way that a fire would ensure the two targets would die.

These people were a real pain in the ass.

When he reported back to Mavis, she had not been pleased to learn that he hadn't finished the job. Her suggestion was to booby trap the car, it being the only way sure of killing the two that needed killing.

"All right, Wade," she said. "It's time to resort to a bomb. Did you bring the needed materials for building one? As a 'just in case' you couldn't shoot them?

"Ah... no. To be honest, Mavis, I'm not very comfortable with explosives yet." The truth was Wade really hadn't invested much of his time in learning to make and plant a bomb.

"Are you fucking kidding me? Are you saying you don't know how to make a basic pipe bomb? And you thought you wanted to be in the business?"

Wade could've sworn that his phone actually heated up from the swear words she'd yelled at him. He'd been cussed at by experts during a brief tenure in the military, but Mavis was as adept at swearing a blue streak as any drill instructor he'd ever had.

"Honestly, Mavis, bombs are messy and this close to town there's gonna be a lot of collateral damage." Wade liked to think of himself as a precision instrument, not a splatter killer. "They're in there, I'll pick them off in the morning. Just a slight delay."

"I want them dead tomorrow, Wade. No more delays, no more excuses. If you want to be paid a decent rate, you need to be efficient. So far, I'm not seeing it."

"Tomorrow they're toast. Just you wait and see." He said, using his most conciliatory tone.

"Make. It. Happen!" The phone went silent. She'd hung up on him.

It was decided. He'd wait until Crow and Fernandez showed themselves. The moment they were away from people, their goose would be cooked.

———

Timothy landed at Tampa International Airport after a grueling red-eye flight from London. After the tedious slog the length of the facility and the slow-moving tramway to the car rental, he set off to find the Hilton in Oldsmar.

Normally, a member of the Association who was on an assignment flew by private charter, allowing said member to bring their arsenal and tools along without scrutiny. That Timothy had been required to fly commercial was a measure of just how irritated the board was with Marjory, and by extension, himself. Fortunately, he was still able to use his organization's resources. In the morning, he'd drive an hour north to a dry cleaners, give the proper identification and be allowed access to an Association equipment stash to arm himself for the unpleasantness ahead.

The other boon that they'd allowed him was access to not only Marjory's electronics, but more importantly the phone of the poor unfortunate she'd co-opted into her ill-advised scheme. He knew right where both the nouveau-assassin and the prey he was following were.

The prey was unimportant. The Association didn't care about them one way or another, other than as a gauge to show Marjory's ability to get the job done. And she'd certainly screwed that up. She was still sitting clear across the country from the ones she'd said she was going to kill.

Disappearing Marjory was a priority, but right now, getting rid of the fool Marjory had hired was priority one.

37

Rosa and I were up early the next morning. We sat on the small porch of our cabin, sipping coffee and looking out over the bay. Seagulls, egrets, and the ever-present ospreys were in major food-gathering mode. An osprey flew overhead hauling a fish that looked almost too big to carry.

In keeping with the plan, we were leaving in twenty-four hours. While we sipped our coffee, we were using the time to decide how to spend our only full day in the area.

"I kinda feel like we've seen the town," Rosa said. "Unless you want to do your running into town plan."

"Honestly, as much as I want to stay in shape, I'm thinking running out where someone could just drive by and shoot us isn't the best plan," I replied. "There's a little out-of-the-way breakfast place called Annie's Cafe I'd like to try, then maybe we could go to the nature preserve, if you're amenable?"

"Might as well. I have to warn you though, Mac. After yesterday's news about not finding any trace of our stalker back home, I'm gonna be carrying under my jacket. It's probably against the rules there, but I'm willing to take a fine if it means I can defend myself if needed."

"No argument here. I'll be packin' right next to you."

Rosa sighed. "I think I'd really like this place, if I wasn't feeling the need to constantly look over my shoulder."

"Yeah. We're definitely seeing Florida through a glass darkly. Let's go get some breakfast, maybe that'll lighten our mood."

———

We emerged from the small roadside eatery quite well-fed. Annie, if she was indeed one of the cooks, really knew her business. Rosa and I had spent our time there sitting in a corner with a view of the door, but trouble hadn't shown up.

"So, riddle me this, Batman," I said as we got into the CRV. "Howcum breakfast down here cost us about half of what it costs at home? I mean what the heck?"

"Some people say it's Wenatchee's lack of an interstate," Rosa replied. "Costs more to get it to our area of Washington state."

"That doesn't scan. Cedar Key is just as far off the beaten path as Wenatchee is. I think we've just gotten used to paying high prices for everything. And sometimes you can only find a reasonable price back there if you go way off the beaten path to some really small town that didn't get the memo to gouge all its customers."

"I see. You think Big Restaurant is out to get you, hunh?"

"Just sayin.' Personally though, I blame all the tourists. Leavenworth, Lake Chelan, it's like a bomb made of higher pricing went off in the touristy spots, and all the locals are caught in the collateral damage."

"I might ask you Mac, what exactly are *we* to Cedar Key?"

"But.. Well... Okay. I just think this little diner here didn't get the memo about gouging tourists either."

"Could be."

————

The wildlife refuge was, to put it mildly, swampy.

Rosa and I drove through a dirt loop, looking for interesting things to see amongst the heavy forest, now heavily invested in losing its leaves. The sky was overcast and every so often a light drizzle would help to darken the mood a little more.

We traversed a short, muddy trail on a boardwalk, following signs which kept pointing to a viewing area. I sighed heavily. Finally, we reached the pot of gold at the end of the rainbow.

I shook my head in disbelief at the prize before us: Another large, swampy pond.

"Dang. That was well worth the trip," Rosa muttered.

"Not even any birds singing." I shook my head. "It's the beginning of November. You'd think every bird would've flown south by now. The trees are deserted, except for crows."

"Mac! Is that a gator?" Rosa pointed over at a floating something on the far side of the pond.

"Maybe? Or.. A log? Honestly I can't tell." We watched the object for a while and were rewarded when it finally dove under the surface and reappeared a few feet closer to us. "Yep. Good eye, Rosa."

"At least we can now say we saw an alligator in the wild."

"Okay then. Time to mud-slog back to the car then," I replied, keeping an eye on the large reptile. It seemed to be moving in our direction. We turned back to the trail, looking over our shoulder, and hurried back to the CRV.

We drove to another turnoff that promised a ranger station and hiking trails. We spent a little time talking to the ranger on duty, who was kind enough to hand us a photocopied map with the trail to the river marked on it.

"Sorry it's not that spectacular here right now," he said. "In the spring, there are birds and bird watchers everywhere. At least, this being a weekday, you'll likely have the whole shebang to yourself."

"We saw a gator," Rosa told him. "He really looked like he was intending to get too close. We booked back to the car."

"They don't usually go after humans." The ranger assured her.

"He sure looked like he was coming towards us." I said.

"Well, I wouldn't get in the water with him, but he probably thought you'd be more trouble than you're worth."

We drove the rest of the way to the trailhead, and found the ranger was correct. We were the only car in the lot. We donned our light rain jackets and started down the trail to the river.

"Y'know, I feel like I should be doing better here," I said as we walked down the broad leaf-strewn trail. "I'm not blending with this place at all. I feel like I just don't belong in this landscape."

"Mac. How long have you been roaming the forests and sagebrush back home?"

"Most of my life, I guess," I admitted.

"And you've been here less than twenty-four hours. You always tell me about how you like to sit quietly outside and observe everything going on around you. You've spent a good portion of your life learning all the nuances there, but no time at all learning this place. Seriously, what'd you expect?"

"It's just weird to be outdoors and feel like an alien."

"Now you know how most of us modern humans feel," Rosa said. "Just experience it, don't judge it."

"Are you saying you like it here?" I asked.

"Oh, yeah." Rosa nodded. "I love it. The warm weather. There aren't mountains, but there is a lot more color. And a sort of weirdness and eerie feeling I like. You have to learn to see the beauty in every landscape."

"Truly you are a wise one."

"Never forget it, my Padawan."

The forested land trail gradually switched over to being a 'surrounded by water' trail. I'd felt like an alien, and for good reason: the swamp around us on all sides looked like an alien landscape. Dark, murky unmoving water surrounded us, with strange root-looking wooden 'spikes' sticking up everywhere. I had no idea what these spikes were, not being covered by any of the field guides I'd purchased.

The Spanish moss blowing in the light breeze looking so enchanting on a sunny day in Homosassa, had turned almost funereal against the gray drizzly skies and swamp. The leafless trees didn't help the mood.

We were almost to the river when my tracker eyes alerted me to the danger we were in.

38

Their car is here.

The targets must've taken a hike down the trail, which, fortunately for Wade, was well marked.

This couldn't be more perfect. We're the only ones here. Just like Mavis said, 'get in, do the job and get the fuck out.'

He opened the duffle in the passenger seat. The only thing was... did he want to go plain or fancy? The duffle contained two 9mm pistols, one Plain Jane but efficient, the other dressed to the nines with extensive accessorizing.

Fancy Boy was inserted into a frame that essentially transformed it into a rifle. Even had a laser site, which might come in handy in this gloom. All he had to do was screw on the extender barrel and it was good to go.

Part of him said, "just keep it simple." Plain Jane is easy to conceal. You'll probably be able to just walk up on the marks and 'bang, bang,' all done.

"Guh! This shouldn't be this hard!" Wade warred with himself for a few minutes, knowing full well that time wasted here could be time someone else might show up at the trailhead.

"Fuck it," he said, taking the 'Glock rifle' out of the duffle. He

screwed on the silenced barrel, tested the laser site and pushed in a magazine. Pulling back a lever that activated the 9mm pistol's slide, he chambered a round. Attaching the sling and he cross-bodied the weapon.

Walking past their car, he slipped an air tag with stickum on the underside of it. Mavis had told him to do it 'just in case.' No need for it, but he wasn't gonna argue with her.

"The heat is on," Wade said out loud. The excitement building in his chest began to course through his entire body. He imagined himself glowing with power like some sort of superhero. No one, nothing could stop what was about to happen.

Leaving the car behind, Wade began the hunt.

39

"ROSA! STOP!" Terror shot through me as she plunged forward. She was not a slow-moving person, and I was not in range to grab her arm.

The trail was wide enough that two people could easily walk abreast, and my urgent tone made her freeze in place. I pointed directly ahead of us, less than six feet down the trail.

"What? What are you pointing at, Mac? I don't see anything."

I reached down and picked up a pebble sitting in the copious leaf litter on the trail. I flicked it forward, and it was just enough to get the snake to move slightly. It was tan with brown 'ovals' along its length. Sitting in the leaves, it was just one step away from being invisible.

"Ho... holy shit!!" Rosa said, taking a large step backward.

"Copperhead. Look how well it blends with the leaves. And not polite enough to warn you, like our rattlesnakes back home. That guy'd bite you with no warning whatsoever, I bet."

"Jesus. I almost walked right over it."

"Yeah," I said. "Sneaky, snakey bastard. Let's just move

along this side of the trail. That should give him plenty of room without pissing him off."

We edged to the farther side of the wide trail and Rosa took her boot and scratched an arrow in the trail's leaf litter. "I want to make sure we don't miss him on the way back," she said.

"He doesn't seem inclined to move," I suggested. "I don't think we have to worry about him as long as we stay clear of him."

"Are you sure? Do you know what a copperhead's striking range is?" Rosa asked, disbelieving. "Not to mention how fast it can move towards you?"

"Umm. Let's see, how long is he? Striking range is about two-thirds of his length. He's definitely a grown snake. So, I don't know, maybe two to three feet?"

"Stand back, Mac, and stop looking at him!"

"You asked me a question and I'm trying to answer it."

"I'm not sure you know that much about snakes, Mac. Maybe you need to study up on that." She shook her head, reluctantly adding, "But you are a good tracker."

"Uh, Thanks?"

"If you weren't such a good tracker, we would have blundered right into it," Rosa added. "Maybe we should shoot him?"

I shook my head. "We're literally in his home. If there were other people out here, I might reconsider."

"Shouldn't we chase him away?" Rosa asked.

"I'd scare him off the trail, but I don't want to piss him off and have him come for us. Then we'd have to shoot him," I said. "We'll just be extra careful going back."

We walked on a bit, and watched the alien landscape pass by. Under the gray skies, the swamp water looked black, and all the root spikes seemed designed to grab and stab if you wound up in it.

I began to get the 'tight feeling' in my stomach. The problem with intuition and gut feelings were that they were usually not very specific. Was this from the snake? Was it just the oppressive surroundings? I'd learned to pay attention to gut feelings, warnings that most people ignored.

But sometimes they were frustratingly opaque.

"Rosa, I'm getting the 'oogie' feeling," I admitted. "I don't know what it is, if it's the snake or something else."

There wasn't a moment's hesitation. Rosa reached behind her, pulled out her Glock and chambered a round.

"Honestly. I'm not sure what it is. Could be the snake." I said.

"You said 'oogie feeling,' Mac." She replied. "Experience has taught me that when you say 'oogie feeling' it always translates to something bad. Now that we know that the snake's there, we know to look for it which means it's not a danger. Thus, it's not the problem."

"I don't know..."

Rosa shook her head. "I don't think you're afraid of the snake. You didn't seem afraid of the snake even when it was close to us. I think it's something else."

"I haven't heard any bird alarms, no concentric rings of disturbance." I said. "If I did, then I'd have something more than my gut to go on."

"Maybe it's the quiet before the storm," she said. "Let's be more safe than sorry. Get your Glock ready."

40

This is the best part.

Wade knew in his mind that it was kinda sick, but his heart told him that the hunt for other humans was on. The excitement threatened to overwhelm him.

He moved along at a fast pace, impatience pulling him along. Being this into it probably wasn't professional. Pros were cold, efficient and calculating. He was glad that Mavis wasn't along, monitoring him. She most likely wouldn't have been impressed with this much enthusiasm.

She is one cold bitch.

Wade smiled to himself. That's why I like her.

He couldn't figure why she didn't want this job for herself though. Why would anyone want to give the fun to someone else?

Wade shrugged. "Never mind. More money for me," he said out loud.

Wade imagined himself a tiger, moving along a jungle trail, and he had to admit it wasn't that much of a stretch. This crummy swamp was jungle-like enough, and he was by far the biggest predator in the neighborhood.

He carried his weapon like he'd seen all the pros do in the movies, keeping it high up and ready to shoot at a moment's notice. As the land slid away and the trail continued into the swamp, he grinned.

"Damn this is fun. You can't beat it: carrying a powerful weapon, wearing all the right clothes."

Preparing for the kill.

It was too perfect. The trail, according to the map on the reader board at the trailhead, dead-ended at the river. There was literally no place to run. If they stayed on the trail, he'd run right into them. If they saw him and panicked, they might wind up trying to escape through the swamp, but Wade knew from past experience what a bad idea that would be. They'd be hip deep in mud and murk water before they got five steps from the trail. Easy pickin's.

And what better place to get rid of bodies? Just let 'em sink into the swamp water. His grin widened, and he picked up his pace even more, now almost jogging.

He saw something scraped into the leaves ahead on the trail, and slowed for a moment to see what it was. As he moved forward he felt something thick and rubbery under his foot.

Then he felt the amazing pain in his leg.

Half wrapped around his ankle, was a tan and brown rope, and it had attached itself to his ankle at one end. A fucking snake!

Wade brought the Glock rifle around and fired at his assailant, only to miss. He instinctively kicked the snake away and that pissed off the already angry reptile even more. It lunged back at him, and sank its teeth into his other ankle.

"Bastard!" Wade screamed, and let loose three shots. The stress of the situation put his aim off slightly and one round damn near shot off a toe. The other two did the job however, and the snake bucked as its spine was severed. Wade wanted to kick it again, but common sense prevailed. While the snake tried to crawl away, Wade racked his brain for what to do.

"Okay. Okay, that was a copperhead," he said out loud, his heart beating like a jackhammer. He was feeling intense pain move up his calves. "And he bit me good. Twice. What'd daddy tell me? Hemotoxic,

poisons the blood and tissues. Shit. I gotta get back to the car! Gotta get to a doc."

Suddenly, Wade didn't feel like the great predator any more.

He stumbled back along the way he'd come, the pain creeping up his legs. It probably wasn't a great idea to be using his legs like this, but he needed to get to a hospital. Wade was pretty sure his targets wouldn't carry him back.

It was getting hard to pick up his feet, they hurt so badly. About half way back to the parking lot, he realized that he was having trouble getting air.

"That's not one.. of the symptoms, is it?" he tried to remember what he knew about snake bites. Copperheads were blood poisoners, tissue and blood... unless... Unless you were allergic. "Oh shit."

His throat began to swell. He sure as hell didn't have no epidural-pen.

"I am well and truly fucked," he thought.

―――――

He'd driven most of the night and he was not in a good mood.

Timothy looked at his tracker and made a left turn onto the road for the river trail. He looked with disdain at the area which only promised to get more swampy as he went along. He didn't like swamps. He'd spent too much time in them.

He passed a ranger station, but his tracker indicated the target he was after was farther along. A few minutes later, he came to a trail-head parking lot. There were two cars in it, A Honda CRV and a Jeep.

Driving past the first, he recognized the plates of the two unfortunates Marjory had dedicated herself to eradicating. Deductive reasoning said that the Jeep must belong to Mr. Budget Assassin.

The amateur's car was unlocked, and Timothy found one pistol and extra mags in a bag on the passenger seat. Sitting along the gear shift was the man's phone. He hadn't even password protected it. Sloppy.

Timothy pocketed the phone, checked his own compact, silenced .22 pistol, and moved to the car of the two targets. The vehicle was locked, but the lock picker he used had the door open in less than ten seconds.

The only things inside were two backpacks, and out of a sense of prudence, he put a micro-tracker under some of the webbing on the outside of each pack, then buried one in the paperwork in the glove compartment. He might need to locate these two again sometime.

They might be the key to drawing Marjory out in the open, assuming they weren't already dead.

Timothy started down the trail, intending to come up on the cut-rate killer from behind.

He'd barely gone fifty yards when he heard someone coming the other way. Someone making not the least effort to be quiet. A few moments later a man, youngish, with some sort of stubby military looking rifle/contraption slung over his shoulder stumbled into view. The punk was handsome, with dishwater blond hair and a strong chin. Timothy began to see how he and Marjory had interfaced.

"And it looks like your little fling is going to get you killed, Marjory. Didn't think that through, did you?" he said under his breath.

Timothy shook his head in annoyance. That's not how he'd trained her. And now Marjory's unprofessionalism had put him here in this wretched swamp land.

Seeing the other man's gun, Timothy reached under his jacket for his own. He stopped his draw when the man yelled out for help, and Timothy noted the blueish lips and pale face.

"Snake bit me," He said, his wheezing words barely audible, "Allergic. Anaphylactic. Can't... breath. Help me, please!"

"Oh, my dear boy, that is tragic," Timothy said. He pulled the man's weapon off to no protest. "Let's get that heavy thing off you, shall we... Wade?"

The name had been bandied about in the communication between Marjory, or as she called herself before this poor twit, "Mavis." The fair-haired muscle-builder barely reacted to a stranger knowing who he was.

"Now, now, old fellow, hunching over like that compresses your lungs. It will help your breathing if we stand you up straight. Good, good. Get those lungs extended a little, that will help some." As Wade stood straight, his back slightly arched, Timothy savagely drove the palm of his hand into the space just under the center of the ribcage, rupturing his target's diaphragm.

Wade dropped like a sack of potatoes, not able to draw breath at all. He looked up into Timothy's indifferent face as if to ask "why?," then dropped onto the ground, spasming. The blow might not've been fatal if the subject hadn't already been half strangled by his allergic reaction. As it was, the young fool would asphyxiate before Timothy could walk back to his rental car.

"Well, that's part one done," Timothy said. "Now, I need to take care of your mistress." He started to pick up Wade's weapon, then paused. He needed to smoke Marjory out. He knew roughly where she was, though not precisely. He needed bait. Looking down the trail, he smiled. He left the gun where it lay, then added Wade's cell phone to the trash lying on the ground.

Hopefully, these young people, if they were still alive, would come to the right conclusions. If they realized they could find Marjory through this phone... After all, they were, according to his research, bounty hunters...

It was a distinct possibility they'd decide to become assassin hunters.

It was a long shot, but it cost him nothing. And if these two simply went deeper into hiding, nothing was lost. If Marjory could find them, he certainly could too, assuming he needed to tie up loose ends later where they were concerned, he could kill them then.

If his ploy didn't work, he'd just have to work a little harder to smoke Marjory out into the open.

41

Rosa and I were on high alert. We'd heard the shots and both had our weapons ready. My arms were crossed, and my Glock was tucked under an armpit, the barrel sticking out backwards, while Rosa's was inside her small sling bag, ready to be pulled out at a moment's notice.

The only reason we were making any effort to hide our defensive measures was that we didn't know who was out there. My gut said it was someone dangerous, but probability said it might be the ranger, or another well-armed hiker. Either way, we didn't want to be seen as being ready to start the shootout at the OK Corral.

"Here's my arrow in the dirt," Rosa said. "Look. A couple of casings on the ground right here. You think whoever it was found the snake?"

"Theory confirmed," I said, pointing out the corpse of the snake on the side of the trail. "Look at these marks. Whoever it was stepped on the snake, then lunged backward. Big scuff here intersects in the dirt with the snake's sign. He must've kicked it. Then shot it." I looked down the trail toward the cars. "I think he got bit."

"How do you know?"

"Look at these big long scuffs through the leaves. Moving with some speed. The tracks say 'haste' to me."

"And what better reason to hurry back toward the parking lot than being snake bit." Rosa said. "Let's follow him. We may need to render first aid."

"Do we even have anything with us for snake bite?"

"If nothing else, we can drive the poor bastard to the nearest hospital." She replied. "Unless it turns out the person bitten was following us to assassinate us. In that case, they can fend for themselves."

"Um, do you even think this might be the person after us?" I considered. "I mean, Ed was pretty sure it was a woman."

"Don't know. Either way, I don't think he poses much threat in the condition he is in now." She shrugged. "Anyway, we're armed and he's compromised."

We followed the increasingly obvious tracks along the trail back. Eventually, the person in front of us began weaving, their feet dragging more and more as they neared the lot.

"They're in a bad way," Rosa said. "Even I can see their tracks now, and they're not picking up their feet at all. Just dragging them along. They fell here, that's a definite hand print."

We were nearing the parking lot, and the track trail was just a series of long scrapes at this point. As we emerged from the forest, we came upon the owner of the tracks, lying face down. Rosa reached down to his neck and checked for a pulse. After a few moments, she looked at me and shook her head.

"Definitely not a threat."

"That's weird," I said. "A cotton mouth is definitely venomous, but the venom shouldn't have taken him out like this. From everything I've read, you usually have time to get to a hospital and get some anti-venom. Amputations, maybe, but not death this quickly."

Rosa had checked both of the man's sock-less ankles. Both legs were purple-ish with dark red blotches. "Looks like he got bit twice. Could that have done it?"

"I'm not sure, but looking at his face, his lips and eyelids are blueish," I said. "Doesn't that kind of indicate asphyxiation?"

"Allergic? Anaphylactic shock?" Rosa said.

"That'd be my guess, but I'm no medical expert."

"You wouldn't think that would've taken him out this fast either. But whatever happened, I'm thinking that our worst fears have been confirmed." I started to reach down for the strange small rifle laying next to the man.

"Mac! Don't. Leave it where it is. We need to get going. I don't want this connected to us in any way. Assuming this guy was here to kill us, I think we need to stay mobile. Getting involved with the authorities will tie us down and give whoever's after us time to catch up."

"What? You don't think this guy's the one who's been after us?"

"He might have been after us. But, if he was, someone else is behind it." Rosa pulled out her gloves and fished the assassin's wallet out as she spoke. "He's local. Key Largo. I have gut feelings too, Mac. And I think this dude's not the one that put the bomb under my car."

"Can we take this?" I said, pointing to his cell phone. "Might be we could learn something. We can ditch it later."

"Risky. First of all, an associate of the dead man could track us with the phone. Second of all, we could be considered a murder suspect carrying the phone of the dead man. Especially if we don't report the death." She shook her head.

"We need answers. And the phone may have them. I

think it's a risk we have to take. We can't run the rest of our lives."

"Okay, but we need to ditch it soon." Rosa bit her lip. "You have a bandana?"

"Always," I replied. Rosa picked up the phone and placed it in the bandana, stuffing both into her sling bag.

Having so much macro information can make a tracker miss micro information. We were moving toward our car to get outta Dodge when I noticed the other tracks.

"Rosa. There was someone else here."

"What? You're sure? What am I saying? It's tracks, of course you're sure."

I dropped down slightly, and the depressions in the gravel stood out in sharp relief. Aside from the indentations they left, there was a slight "shininess" on the individual pebbles where their normal grime had been wiped away. It was subtle, but if you know what to look for...

"Two sets of tracks, no... three. Two coming this way, one walking back."

We walked to the far end of the lot, where a lone Jeep sat. I looked in without touching anything, and put my own gloves on. With the door open, I saw the duffle with the other pistol in it. Mr. Two Guns could've just been a casual gun nut, but I didn't believe that for an instant.

The last set of tracks went on a little farther and disappeared where a set of tire tracks showed that someone had backed out and left from the exit. I couldn't tell in the gravel what kind of car it was.

"There was definitely someone else here," I said. "They saw the guy. Their tracks were right next to him. They left him there."

"Maybe on their way to better cell coverage? Gone to get help?" Rosa asked. "In which case, someone will be here soon."

"Maybe that was it. Or maybe they just didn't want to get involved."

"Either way, I want to get gone, Mac. As in right now." Rosa said. *"Vamanos!"*

I didn't think it would look good to flee the scene of a possible murder. Not very courageous either. I was a little ashamed.

But I didn't want our hands tied now either.

There was so much that didn't make sense, and we needed to get to the bottom of it.

———

We debated for some time, as we drove, if we wanted to go back to the cabin and get our stuff. There was no guarantee that someone wouldn't be waiting there for us. In the end, we decided there was nothing there that we couldn't do without or replace.

We'd made it a habit to keep most of our essentials in the go-bags that Uncle Gil had given us, and our cash and cards were in the sling bags we carried with us. A trip to Walmart would resupply us without too much trouble or even expense.

I was driving. When we met State Route 24, I turned in the opposite direction from Cedar Key and headed toward the interstate. Rosa pulled her pack into the passenger seat from the back and began fishing around in it.

"We need to find a place to park, and check out Two-Gun's phone," I said. "It came on when we picked it up, and it's not protected. Maybe we can get some answers. You'd think a guy that killed people would at least put a password on his phone."

"You don't," Rosa said. "Tell me why your phone back home doesn't have a password."

"Well.. I guess I don't like the hassle of having to put in a code every time I want to look something up," I admitted.

"Well then, let this be a lesson to you, my poor innocent little lamb," she said. "I'd guess that the reason this phone is unlocked is probably very similar, and now we're going to steal all the information on it before I send it into a trashcan somewhere."

"I'll be pass-wording the shit out of every device I own after this."

Rosa patted me on the leg. "See? You can be trained. Anyway, I'll start checking this phone out while you drive. I'll tell you what I find as we go along."

We turned south when we hit the interstate, heading in the general direction we'd come from.

"Yep. He was definitely after us," Rosa said. "I'm in his messages and someone named "Mavis" hired him to kill us. Evidently, they had a history. Want to know how much your life is worth, Mac?"

I looked at her with a pained expression. "Okay?"

"She hired him for twenty grand. I guess that's good money for murdering random people. She also mentioned that she's as far from Florida as you can get in the continental U.S."

"In other words, the Evergreen State. Diagonally opposite across the nation from the Sunshine State."

Rosa stopped scrolling and looked out the window for a moment. "Still no cops."

"It feels odd for someone to not be chasing us. Assuming they're not."

"The death was on a state preserve," Rosa said. "The state highway patrol would've probably been the ones handling it. I haven't seen any units on the way at this point." She stared out at the passing palmettos for a moment. "But doesn't that say to you that the second person at the trailhead didn't call the cops?"

I nodded. "Right. And that maybe he or she killed off the blonde Adonis?"

"Maybe. That death shouldn't have happened." Rosa shook her head. "So, if they did somehow kill that guy, why didn't that second person come and attack us? Are they friend or foe?"

"This just keeps getting more and more complicated," I replied. "Keep scrolling."

Rosa scrolled through the messages, looking for any information that we could use, when a message popped into existence.

"Wade, you were supposed to keep in touch. Is the job done? - Mavis"

We looked at each other, nonplussed.

"I can see that their car is moving. Did you take their car? Talk to me!"

"Shit!" I said. "She's been tracking us the whole time!" I felt the anger growing in my chest. Just when I didn't think I could get any angrier.

"I am really sick of this bitch," Rosa said. "I'd really like to shoot her in the face." Her voice had almost come out as a growl.

"Well, my love, maybe it's time we went back and did that very thing," I said. "I am sick of her too, and I'm sick of running. This could go on the rest of our lives, and to be honest, I feel like doing something truly stupid."

"Gil's original plan? Draw her out and ambush her? Stupid or not, that plan has really grown on me."

"Me too. It's time to go home." I said, "but maybe we need to send a message first."

42

He was trying to drive her insane.

Wade's sudden turn of not answering her immediately was not a good sign, and Marjory began to have a bad feeling about the whole thing. It irritated her that she was a professional killer who nonetheless was nervous about how this whole thing had turned out.

Of course, the nervousness was a relatively new thing. It started the day she'd been called to meet with Timothy.

She looked over at the small case on her nightstand. It would be really nice to have a little "sumpthin' sumpthin'" to take the edge off, but this was not the time. This could be the end game. Wade could just be away from his phone, but why would he be driving the target's car now?

The most likely answer, if her protege was any good at all, was that he was moving bodies. No one with any sense would use their own vehicle to transport a bloody corpse or two if they could use the victim's. But, the meeting between Wade and young Mac Crow would've essentially been in a swamp, nature preserve be damned.

So why bother to move the bodies? Just sink 'em.

If moving the bodies was the case, she'd have to have a talk with him about... No. Scratch that. If he'd been successful, she'd need to fly down there as fast as possible and make sure that Wade disappeared without a trace. As far as the Association was concerned, he'd have never existed and all the 'glory' would be hers.

They'd reinstate her, and her life would be golden again. She'd once more be one of the killer elite.

But if everything was going all right, then why the hell was Wade driving so far to get rid of the bodies?

43

"So, we're agreed," Rosa said. "We both want to go home and draw this Mavis out and, assuming that we have no other choices, kill her."

"Jesus. It sounds so cold-blooded, doesn't it?" I said.

"If the opportunity comes up to slam her face into the ground and zip tie her six ways to Sunday, I'd certainly be willing to turn her over to the cops. Thing is, she's supposedly a professional."

"No amateur could've tracked us this far," I replied. "And the fact that there was more than one of them... Are we sure the guy at the trail head was out to kill us?"

"It was a nature preserve, Mac," Rosa said. "No hunting there, at least no hunting of animals. He was after us. I'd bet everything I own."

"And we can't give her any chance at all," I said. "Hopefully, after it's all over, there'll be enough evidence of what we're up against that it'll be obvious self defense."

Rosa shrugged her shoulders. "If there's not when it's over, there will be soon after. Shall we call Steve?"

I nodded. "We're not telling him our plan, right? We tell

him, he'll tell Uncle Gil and I'm pretty sure that we'll have everyone mobilized. This woman probably has enough surveillance on our family that she'll be cautious as hell if it looks like they're ready to go to war. We want her confident, and if a pro-killer ever is such, overconfident."

"Plus, I just really would like to keep the Fam out of the line of fire with this one," Rosa said. She reached into her Go-Bag and pulled out a pre-paid phone, still in its package. Unlike the iPhones Steve has supplied us with, it was a flipper, one of the ones that had been in the bag when Uncle Gil had handed them to us. She pulled it out of the packaging, went through the activation procedure and dialed Steve's number.

"Hey. It's Carmen," she said. "Need to keep this brief. We're burned. Consider your comms compromised. We are going rogue in the wild wild west. No. No! We think this is the best way."

Rosa listened for a moment, nodded, then said; "So let it be written, so let it be done. Where can we leave the car? You won't hear from us again, unless everything is resolved. Goodbye, and thanks for everything."

She closed the phone and put it back in the pack. We looked at each other for a moment. This was it. We were free in the wind now, completely on our own.

"What's next?" I asked.

"Steve wants us to leave the car in the Walmart parking lot in Chiefland, so we need to be going North."

"Probably be best if we went analog after that," I said. "We can see if there's a local shopper or newspaper where we can find someone selling a car. If she's able to track us still, I don't want to get off a plane in Sea-Tac and wind up dead as soon as we leave the airport. A different car will at least cure however she was able to track this one."

"Sounds like a plan," Rosa replied. "I'm paranoid about

even using an Uber at this point. I'm eternally grateful to Gil that he made sure we were well-supplied with cash."

"We have to assume that even our new identities are compromised. We've been using the cards at our lodgings."

"Remember, Mac, with this, right now she knows where we are. We might as well stock up on supplies before we leave Florida. We can stop using the cards on the road back. Once we go analog, driving a different car she won't know where we are."

"All right then, let's go to Chiefland and go car shopping."

———

We did pay cash for our ride. A car was the one thing we wanted to be untraceable. The seventy-something lady who sold us her slightly dented 2006 Subaru forester wagon was more than happy to let it go for $3500 and hand us the title. We took all the paperwork, signed by both parties and assured her we'd take it all and file it with the Florida DMV.

I don't like fibbing to old ladies.

We stuffed all the paperwork, signed with our real names, into the glove compartment to take care of later. Right now, we didn't want the transaction to show up in any database.

Rosa dropped me off a block from the Walmart where we'd parked Steve's car, and I walked back and cleared all our gear out. While at a rest stop, we'd gone over everything we had with a fine-toothed comb to make sure that there were no air-tags or electronic trackers. We hadn't found a damn thing. I scooped up both Go-Bags and a laundry bag with our gun accessories, left the two phones Steve had given us under the driver's seat, along with the keys, and locked it up.

Walking the block back to our new, used car, I dumped our gear in, along with what we'd bought at Walmart, and climbed in the passenger seat.

"Only one thing left to do," Rosa said, handing me Wade's phone.

"Time to declare war," I replied.

44

It took her a while to realize that her phone was ringing. Her grogginess evaporated when she saw who was calling.

"Wade! Gawdammit! Where the hell have you been?" she yelled.

The voice that replied was not Wade's, though it seemed familiar.

"Wade's most likely in the morgue at this point, Mavis. He made a run at us, but it didn't turn out well for him. Sorry."

She was still coming down, so it took a moment for the dots to connect. When they did, a surge of adrenaline brought her fully alert.

"MacKenzie Crow. You little shit. I guess you're not quite the sheep I thought you were. I'm surprised that you had the balls to call me and gloat, though. I think I've shown you what I'm capable of."

"Yeah. We understand now that you're a big bad. Mind if I ask just how we got on your bad side?"

"Tell me where you are... ah... I see that you're still in Florida. Stay put, and I'd be glad to come there and give you all the details, MacKenzie."

"No need to trouble yourself. We're coming to you. Can't say for sure when or how exactly we'll arrive, but both Rosa and I are tired of running."

"So... what? You're just gonna come here like good little lambs.

Like maybe that'll buy you some mercy? You don't really seem that dumb."

"Well, you see Mavis, that's not our plan. We're coming back to get you off our back. Permanently. Do I need to say that any plainer? From what I've read, you killers like to speak in metaphors."

Marjory sat back on the bed. The brass balls on this kid! But... what a fucking idiot! Did he think this was an action movie and he was the star?

"I get your meaning, MacKenzie. It's all I can do to keep from laughing, but I don't want to discourage you. You come on home, Rambo, and we'll have this out. If you're serious."

"I'm serious."

"It occurs to me, that this might be a trick. You might be blowing smoke up my ass so that you can buy time to get on a boat to Costa Rica."

"I told you, we're coming!"

"You'd better, little man. Because if you don't, here's what's going to happen. Your Uncle? I'll blow his balls off from a thousand yards away and he can die bleeding out in agony. Your friend Vinnie? Blown to bits? The two old people at the farm? Burned up in their beds. And don't get me started on what I'll do to your Mommie Dearest. It involves duct tape and a baseball bat, and it'll take a long time and a lot of screaming. You get the picture?"

Silence on the phone. Then, "I get it."

"You try and play me, MacKenzie, they all get it. They're my hostages, and they don't even know it. You can try and warn them, but if they show even the slightest indication of fortifying or bugging out, I'll show you what I'm really ready to do to fulfill my contract."

"We're low on cash. We have to drive back, and from Florida that'll take a good five or six days. Then we can finish this."

"I don't see you here by a week from today, I start killing them all. See you soon, MacKenzie."

"Yes. You will."

———

Timothy looked at the icon on his phone, indicating he had a voice mail. That was an unlikely event on this particular phone, as it was the one he was using to spy on Marjory. The voice mail would be a very accurately transcribed copy of a call to Marjory's phone.

Curious, he hit the play icon, and listened to her discussion with young Crow.

"Well," he said to himself, "someone's getting a bit cocky." The two young people had come to the conclusions he'd wanted, but as a bonus, instead of going on the run, they were going to try and draw Marjory out themselves. An extremely ill-advised move, but one which would benefit him greatly in trying to smoke out his ex-pupil.

He pulled out his iPad, and looked for the trackers he'd placed in their gear. He was surprised to find two of the trackers, he assumed the backpacks, were heading generally north, toward the panhandle. The third was stationary in a small town at a... yes.. a Walmart.

He changed searches, and found the would-be assassin's phone. It was sitting not far away from the latter micro-tracker. He assumed they'd ditched it, most likely into a nearby trash can. The two phones that Marjory had been using to track her quarry were also in the same spot as the third micro-tracker, the one in their car.

The only conclusion was that these two young people, who Marjory had built her plan on to get back in the Association's good graces, were getting smart. They'd evidently switched rides and gone dark. If he hadn't so carefully hidden his devices in their personal gear, they would be well and truly off the radar. Timothy found himself impressed.

He wondered if Marjory was in as strong a position as she assumed she was.

45

We were on the longest road trip ever.

We'd decided that using any kind of public transportation was out of the question, because we didn't want Mavis to know exactly where we were, or exactly when we were arriving. That's why we'd pulled the stunt of buying the ladie's car with cash and not registering it.

We were driving the big diagonal across the continental U.S. from Florida to Washington State. It would take us a while, but as long as we were moving, it was going to be impossible for our assassin to find us, much less intercept us on the way, a trick I wouldn't put past her.

Taking turns, we left Florida, passed through Georgia, then Mississippi, then Louisiana, hugging the Gulf of Mexico as much as possible. Any other time we'd have been stopping constantly, trying to not miss the interesting scenery and attractions of these southern states. In our current states of mind, they were just places to get through as quickly as possible.

By the time we were a quarter of the way across Texas, both Rosa and I were so tired that an accident was sure to happen if we didn't pull over. Fortunately, Texas has more than a few giant truck stops.

At the time we pulled into a stop prosaically named "the Big Gas," it was past midnight. Rosa and I hadn't eaten for hours. We first went to the restaurant and were pleasantly surprised by the burgers we ordered. It's hard to screw up a hamburger, but I've definitely eaten at places that managed to. This burger was actually quite tasty, though truth be told, we were starving. There's no more tasty sauce than hunger.

Having full bellies brought its own consequences. Already dead for need of sleep, we barely made it back to the Subaru and reclined our seats before Rosa, her jacket pulled over her like a blanket was softly snoring. As I lay there in the reclined driver's seat, my mind tried to go over what we'd do when we got home, but I firmly put it out of my mind. Instead, I imagined myself lying against a cool rock by a river, a fire crackling nearby. The more effort I put into making the image seem real, the farther I drifted through the veils to finally arrive at the land of Morpheus.

———

The next morning, after breakfast, we were on our way, the high speeds allowed on the Texas freeway system moving us through the Lone Star state with terrible haste. Texas is damn big, and from what I saw on our route, damn flat. I missed my mountains.

Splitting the driving chores, we covered a lot of ground though. Nonetheless, we had to stay at a small mom and pop motel when we made it to the New Mexico border. Texas had taken us fourteen hours of steady driving to make it across the entire state, and that was driving on the interstate.

I don't remember that much about the motel. Rosa and I were both so tired when we made it to our room, we were barely able to shower without falling asleep standing up. Seconds after we were in bed, covers pulled up, we were dead asleep.

Next morning, we had a tasteless breakfast that even hunger couldn't improve. Once back on the highway, we turned north, bypassing all the scenic beauty of New Mexico at high speed. Colorado wasn't much better. Lots of stunning natural beauty that we barely commented on.

Normally, I'd have been enchanted by all this wonder, all these places I'd only seen photos of, but both Rosa and I were hanging under the pall of what we were about to attempt when we got home. Rosa, ever the better tactical thinker, decided enough was enough.

"Mac, our route takes us toward Salt Lake City, and Moab isn't far off the way. I want to stop over there for a day."

"Maybe it's better if we just keep going, Rosa. I want to get this over with as soon as possible."

"I understand that. But we are tense, and we are fried. We need to take a day off, get our minds right and then move on toward the finish line. The way we are now, or at least the way I feel, I think we could easily make errors that could cost us our lives. I don't want to be a pushy bitch about it, but we need to turn off to Moab."

"All right. I trust your judgment. Moab it is."

"Bueno."

46

Timothy had followed the two young lovebirds half-way across Texas. They drove like they had a purpose, only stopping when they absolutely had to. Eventually, when he was sure they were heading back home, he turned off toward Dallas. There was no need to drive the entire way when he could simply fly to Seattle and drive a much shorter distance to their destination.

His tools of the trade, he shipped ahead of him, though if necessary, he could buy new weapons. It was America, after all.

A new disturbing development had arisen, however. Marjory's devices had gone 'off the grid,' no trace of them. She'd finally gotten smart and either slipped them into a Faraday pouch or had a safe house that was somehow shielded. At least it was good to know that she hadn't forgotten everything he'd taught her.

He turned in his rental at DFW and booked a first-class seat on a late-night flight to Seattle. Timothy, especially when on assignment, was a man who traveled lightly, almost to the point of minimalism. He carried no weapons into the airport, not even a Swiss Army knife in his small backpack. He would've breezed through TSA in short order if he hadn't been behind people who evidently had never flown before or were more likely simply morons.

He wasn't the sort of man who became frustrated easily, having invested a great deal of time in meditative practices, but as he watched the couple in front of him fumble with their equipment, have to throw away water bottles and too large shampoos and make-up items in the trash, to have to spend an inordinate amount of time fishing their electronics from deep in their carry-ons, he felt his composure slipping. Finally, the agent from the opposite line signaled him to switch lines, as that second line emptied out while his own line suffered constipation.

The rest of the trip was uneventful, and Timothy used the time to get some much needed sleep. World class assassin or not, he'd been flying and driving for the last several days with little rest. He awoke, bemused, as the plane landed at Seattle Tacoma International Airport. Perhaps not the best operational security on his part, but it was what it was. The British military had taught him to sleep when the opportunity arose.

Renting a car, he made his way through the light morning traffic of Seattle, turned onto Interstate 90 and began the journey to this small mid-state town called Wenatchee.

"I'll see you soon, Marjory," he said to himself, "and all your mistakes and foolishness will come home to roost. Possibly my own as well."

47

Moab is amazing.

We drove into town late in the afternoon and were stunned by the sunlight running along the tops of the red rock mountains that surround the town. I'd wanted to come here for a long time, but work had always seemed to get in the way. If we'd known what we were missing (photos couldn't begin to do the area justice) both Rosa and I agreed we'd have made time. My only regret was that we were here to recharge and plan more than we were here to sight see.

We drove into the town proper, one side of the valley glowing with early evening sunlight, the other in deep purple shadow, and stopped at the Moab Diner for dinner. Rosa had a steak, while I opted for fish and chips.

The difficult part was finding a place that would take cash without running a credit card. We found a little place attached to a restaurant a few miles out from the town itself that was willing to play along and we had a place to sleep. I don't know how many stars the place would have had on a review site, but it was clean, warm and the bed was soft. No cold October drafts either.

Next day, we ate very lightly and took a run into town, leaving the Subaru at our hotel. It'd been several days since we'd run, and the first half mile was, to say the least, clumsy. We were running on a path that paralleled the road, dust puffing up from our trail runners. Rosa had on a tight-fitting winter weight lycra number, which accentuated her form very nicely. Hopefully I can be forgiven for lagging behind simply to get a better view.

I was dressed in a baggy gray Walmart sweats with a thick gray sweatshirt. If I'd had the right wool cap, I could've auditioned for the remake of Rocky.

We jogged on through Moab, and headed out of town on the other end. Though the landscape was very different, the vibe was tourist chic, very much like the "Bavarian village" of Leavenworth, just a short ways away from my home. We passed a lot of trinket and souvenir shops.

We met the Moab Canyon Pathway at the Colorado River and ran through gorgeous cliffscapes along the highway, turning around at the entrance to Arches National Park. We stopped when we arrived back in Moab proper, the warming day evaporating the sweat on our faces.

"Oh Lord," I said, "that felt good."

"Yes. I haven't felt my body let go of tension like this since Homosassa," Rosa replied. "Why don't we get something to eat, and maybe now we're in a good head space to strategize."

We stopped at a little cafe, an eclectic place selling not only food, but a lot of different home-made trinkets. We found a table outside to eat, and once done, basked in the warming day.

"Considering what we're planning is very illegal," Rosa said, breaking the contented silence, "we're going to need to lure her to someplace isolated."

"Maybe we *should* get the local sheriffs involved. We could be the bait, the law could nab her when she came for us."

"I know you don't want to shoot this woman, Mac, hell bitch that she is. But the problem with getting the cops to 'help' us is that we lose control of the situation. They may decide to go with a plan that we don't agree with, and completely screw up our chance to get a shot at her. Also, we'd be placing our lives in the hands of a department of overworked, overstretched law officers, and expect them to have the same skin in the game that we do. I'm not sure I wanna take that particular risk, particularly when the Fam's safety is on the line too. I think we're only going to get one chance at this."

My gut said she was right. "All right. If we're going to lure her in, it seems to be that the best place would be my place. I know every square inch of the area. It's my home turf. It reminds me of a story Sensei Dade told me about not following the rules in a fight. He got into another martial art style for a while and was wailed on by a senior student in that dojo. He finally changed the rules, and took the other person down hard."

"Did he get a belt in that other system?" Rosa asked.

"No... he was kicked out. He told me that if he'd been on his own turf, his own dojo, he'd have never had to do any of it. I'll tell you the story some time, but here it applies to us in that we have a much better chance on our own turf."

"We'll control the rules of engagement."

"I think we'll have a much better chance of not dying. And while we're there, we can set up a few surprises."

"That's good," Rosa said. "Because I think we're going to need every advantage we can get."

———

The final leg home was uneventful.

The road from Moab to Salt Lake was one of the more god-awful landscapes I'd ever seen. It was like driving through a gravel pit for mile after mile.

We drove through Salt Lake City traffic, seeing little of the city or even of the lake itself, and on to Idaho.

I often wonder what people from other countries, playing tourist in the U.S., think about the vastness of America. I could see how the peoples who were here before the white man could've considered it a paradise, even while living with all the hazards of nature. We were moving along at seventy miles per hour most of the way, and still the road and all that surrounded it seemed to go ever onward.

The only way we kept driving was alternating drivers while the other rested. We crossed from Oregon to Washington State and kept driving. Part of our Walmart splurge before we'd left Florida was for camping equipment. It'd been intended for use in case we weren't able to find a motel that'd take cash. It turned out that there were still enough motel owners with the entrepreneurial spirit, that believed in hard currency, that the issue hadn't come up.

We were within ten miles of Wenatchee when we pulled into a small family owned RV park that offered tent sites. Pulling the tent and sleeping gear out of their packaging for the first time, we set up and prepared for possibly the last good night's sleep of our lives.

Tomorrow, Operation Final Stand would begin, and knowing it might be our last time, Rosa and I made love. Very enthusiastically. The neighbors were probably scandalized.

Early the next morning, we stopped at an office store, made a few purchases, including a small metal file box, then went to the bank where our safety deposit boxes were. We grabbed our phones, stuffed them in the metal box and headed for my trailer along the Columbia.

It was time to prepare the battleground.

48

She'd let herself slip for a while.

Marjory, realizing that she had nothing she could do until the prey came to her, had decided that worrying was useless. Young MacKenzie Crow and his little Mexican chica would either show up to have this out, or they'd lose their nerve and head for parts unknown. She no longer had a way to track them.

Every once in a while, she'd pull her electronics out of her pouch, fire them up and see if there was anything new from MacKenzie's associates, some new bit of surveillance that would indicate that her prey had come home for help.

She doubted that they'd flown. It was almost impossible to fly anymore without pinging the grid, credit cards being the main form of payment the airlines accepted. A person could pay with cash, but it'd set so many alarm bells off with the authorities it would be like a flare. A flare that would compromise any attempt at anonymity.

They could've lied and be coming by train, but Marjory felt that after trying to maintain their cagey attempts at hiding, the likely bet was that they actually were driving.

"When these kids show up, I'm going to have to hunt them like one of the old-time lion hunters," she thought. "If I go to them, I can

expect an ambush or a sting. Either them trying to be action heroes or getting the cops to lie in wait for me. Reconnaissance will be the key."

But one way or another there would be a reckoning. Part of her said that her attempt at reinstatement was doomed. That she should just fade away now. But a stronger part wanted to kill this fucking kid. He'd beaten her best efforts so far, and that attacked who she was, her personal and professional identity.

She would kill him for that.

———

She was replacing her devices in the pouch when she heard the sound.

She raised her device to her eye level, and what she found greatly surprised her.

Crow's iPhone had activated. Switching to mapping, she was stunned to find that not only had her quarry stealthed in, they'd managed to grab their phones and keep that hidden until they could get back out of town.

It was a trap; that couldn't be more obvious. There was no way, being cognizant of how trackable cell phones were, that they'd suddenly gotten careless. They were telling her that if she wanted them, she'd have to come onto their home ground and take her chances.

What to do was obvious, how to do it, a lot less so. Marjory went to a back closet of the hotel room and pulled out two large cases. Opening one, she saw a large scoped rifle. Opening the other, she saw various small arms.

What was best? Stealthing in with the sniper outfit, or going in, guns blazing, and overwhelming them with superior firepower.

Perhaps a little bit of both.

49

We were as set as we were going to be. I looked at Rosa and she nodded. I plugged my iPhone into the charger sitting in my Airstream.

"From everything Steve told us, as soon as it has enough charge to reactivate the phone, she'll know it's been moved from the safety deposit box." I said, whispering.

"And once she knows that," Rosa said, just as quietly, "she'll be able to track it right here, and we'll be waiting for her. Honestly, though, Mac, maybe we should have either stopped by Gil's place or the gun safe in the office. Our M-4's would be a lot better to defend with than a pair of Glock pistols and an antique Winchester." The lever-action rifle was the one I'd appropriated from the cache of a dead man.

"If she's keeping an eye out for us, you know those places would be somehow surveilled. I'm pretty sure if we'd gone to a gun shop that she'd have known through whatever electronic magic she's using to keep tabs on us because of the registration with the state. Our only chance is for her to think we don't know she's coming. Now, we need to get back to our hiding spot before she does. You can see the trailer from the cliffs, but you can't see our spot behind the shed. If she comes to the driveway, she'll see our two surrogates and hopefully, while she's dealing with them, we can return the favor."

"If she doesn't have some sort of bug in this place we couldn't find, Mac. She may be close already."

I glanced at the karate kicking dummy I'd borrowed from the shed out back and the hat mannequin that Rosa had paid cash for at the Habitat for Humanity store. Both were made up to resemble us as much as was possible. They sat at the table in front of my largest window. A veiled semi-see-through curtain obscured their details from the outside, but the light from the rear windows made their outline easy to spot. If the assassin came at night, the light over the stove would outline them without giving anything away. Hopefully.

"She's gonna be suspicious of this phone being activated," Rosa said, still whispering "Especially after we went to so much trouble to not use them for the last month or so. But if she wants us, she has to come for us."

"Let's just admit that we're getting desperate," I said. "Hopefully we've thought this through enough."

"Sitting behind the stone shed will give some protection in case she uses explosives. In either case, she's gonna have to come up here to make sure we're dead."

"Hopefully we won't be," I said. "Hopefully it'll be her who gets to go meet God and explain all this."

———

We didn't have as long to wait as I would've thought. There may have been something to what Rosa had said about the trailer being bugged.

She and I had been sitting in camp chairs under the camouflage netting I'd pulled out from my shed, checking our weapons more than was necessary. Above us, a thick overgrowth of cotton wood limbs, leaves already on the ground, protected us from being seen from the cliffs.

It was about six p.m. when I heard the ravens that nested on the cliff face above the ground basalt track that is my driveway start alarming at something. The sun had just gone behind the cliffs above us, but it was still shining on the shore of the river below us.

"Something just set off my neighbor ravens," I said, pointing toward the noise. "Coming down the drive. Unless she has rappelling gear, that's the only way she could come down here."

"I'll bet, assuming that's her, that she's already checked the cliff top for snipers, same as we did earlier," Rosa said, her voice barely above a whisper.

"She'd be a fool if she didn't." I pulled out the small set of binoculars. A silhouette moved through the sagebrush. The shape evolved into a dark-haired woman, both tall and muscular. She wore a black outfit, including military style pants and boots as well as a black baseball cap. I couldn't help but flash back to Sarah Connor in *Terminator 2*.

She stayed low the whole time, not exposing herself to any ambushing fire from the trailer. The only reason I could see her was the bright backlighting of the still sun-lit area across the river.

I pulled out my burner phone to get the sheriffs on the way. To my dismay, there was no signal at all. Normally, with a tower across the river, I'd have four bars.

"Shit. She's jammed or cut off our cell service, somehow!"

"Then we're on our own, Mac. Tell me what she's doing."

"She's kneeling, looking at the trailer with what I assume are a small pair of binoculars."

"Can you see what she's packing?"

She's wearing a tactical vest, lots of pockets," I breathed

into Rosa's ear. "Side arm on her left leg. Big knife on her belt, and... Oh damn! An MP5 it looks like. Shit!"

"We're matching a lever-action antique .30-30 against a modern full-auto weapon. We're gonna have to be very good." Rosa whispered, grim determination on her face. Rosa carried the rifle for the simple reason that she was by far the better shot between us.

She lowered herself into a sitting position and raised the rifle. Rosa only had a sliver of space between the alignment of the end of the Airstream and the edge of the shed. She lowered the rifle.

"Shit!" I barely heard the curse. Looking over her shoulder I saw why she'd said it. The Assassin had circled to the left and had effectively moved out of the line of fire. Rosa looked at her secondary firing position, set behind a pile of lava rock directly behind my trailer. The plan there was to shoot through the open back window, through the front. Hoping of course that Miss Murder Incorporated would walk up to make sure she'd finished the job.

A moment later, the assassin called out to the trailer. "Hey Macccie! I'm home!"

A second later, the MP5 began dismantling my trailer.

The Airstream was designed for living, an artsy mobile domicile that I had painstakingly restored over the years. Its thin aluminum walls were not intended to take punishment of any kind. Certainly not made to withstand a constant assault by high-velocity rounds coming in by the dozens.

Rosa shoved me back behind the stone shed and squirmed right back there beside me. The skin of the trailer was so thin that it did little to slow the momentum of the rounds smashing into it. The back side of my little home erupted with either holes punched all the way through or pimples where bullets had almost made it through both front and back walls.

The shooting seemed to go on forever, and then stopped. "She's switching mags," Rosa said. "It's now or never." Crawling to her secondary position, she raised the Winchester and aimed in the back window, waiting.

Marjory's gleeful-sounding voice came through the silence. "Take that you assholes! This was supposed to be an easy hit, but you caused your dear Marjory no end of trouble." Rosa and I glanced at each other. (Marjory?) The assassin continued. "This job should've been smooth as silk and over weeks ago. You two turned it into a circus! At this point, I'm likely gonna have to go on the run after this clusterfuck. The Association will never take me back now, but at least I finished the stinking job."

Rosa coldly looked down the barrel of her rifle, and with a careful slow pull on the trigger, ended the monologue abruptly. I looked at her face, hoping to see triumph, but her compressed lips told me her shot hadn't been decisive.

A moment later, my fears were confirmed when a screech came from the front: "You bastards! You wanna play games? Well, there's no success like excess!" I heard something smash through the broken window.

Rosa's eyes got big, and she threw herself away from the rock pile. She ran, crouching trying to get back to the shed and almost made it.

50

The explosion sounded like a nuke had gone off at close range. The Airstream lifted off its blocks for a moment, and Rosa fell at my feet, grabbing her thigh.

I didn't think about what had happened. My sole intent in this universe was to get my loved one out of harm's way. I got both my arms under her armpits and dragged her the rest of the way behind the shed. She lifted a bloody hand away from her leg, and I saw the strip of aluminum sticking out of her left quad. Rosa's eyes were tearing up with pain, but she didn't even groan.

A whoosh of flame lifted out of the remains of the trailer and I smelled propane. It had been a miracle the tank hadn't exploded, but now it was doing a good impression of a jet engine through one of the broken pipes for the stove. Everything burnable in the trailer was catching on fire. The wood deck would probably be next.

"Mac," Rosa said through gritted teeth, "she's gonna come back here. She has to if she's thorough. Where's the rifle?"

I looked where she'd been shooting from and saw the Winchester. Having been caught by the blast, it was at the base of a tree. The barrel looked like it was slightly bent and the hammer looked to be hanging out of the back of the rifle. No help there.

"Rifle's broken. How bad is your leg?"

"Hurts like hell, but barely bleeding," She said. "Hopefully we can surprise her with the Glocks."

Or, the assassin would find us and overwhelm us with superior firepower. Most of the pockets on the front of the tactical vest she'd been wearing looked to be magazine sized, and if they were, she wasn't going to run out of bullets before some of us were dead. Even if we got lucky and killed her, the likelihood of both Rosa and I making it was slim. Rosa's life was my priority.

And I had an idea. I knew Rosa would hate it, but I was going to do it anyway. I gave her a very brief run down, knowing that the assassin, probably watching the trailer for signs of life, would be coming soon.

"No Mac! That's a terrible idea; she'll kill you!"

"I'm doing it. If she sees me running away without you, she'll assume you're dead and go after her primary target. I'll slip through the brush along the creek, and when I get enough distance between us, I'll start shooting. She'll chase me for sure."

"No, Mac. Please!"

I took out my Glock from its holster, and was about to move when Rosa grabbed my shirt sleeve. She was reaching, with some pain, toward her right ankle and came up with the small automatic, gaudily colored in sky blue and black.

"Never hurts to have a backup," she said, handing me the compact 9 mm. She pulled me in closer. "Do. Not. Die. Promise me."

"I promise," I told her, having low confidence that I'd be able to keep that promise. "I'm gonna take you down into the brush by the creek. I want you to lie down and hide. For once, Rosa, I need for you to be meek and hidden. If she shows up, don't shoot until you're sure. That vest might have armor plates."

Rosa nodded, and using the cover of the burning trailer, I half-hauled her into the brush and gave her a quick kiss. "I love you," I said.

"I know," she said, quoting one of her favorite movies.

I shook my head and moved out through the undergrowth.

Crawling for the last fifty feet, I emerged onto the dirt road, downriver from the trailer. I'd come out around sixty yards east of my assailant, and through the grass, I could see her putting a bandana on her left arm. She was still using that arm, but not very well, and I could see blood soaking through. Rosa's shot had at least wounded her. The MP5 hung on a sling down her right side, and though I couldn't hear exactly what she was saying, I was sure it wasn't rated PG.

This was the best chance I was going to get. I was a good shot at twenty-five yards, but I was no daisy at all at sixty. I hoped I could pull the shot off. Raising the Glock, I took my time, slowed my breathing and carefully and slowly pulled the trigger, aiming for her upper pectoral area, just above the vest.

I don't know if I didn't allow for windage, or if she turned her body slightly at just the wrong moment. She grabbed her neck, but didn't stagger at all.

"Oh, you son of a bitch!" she screeched. She hooked the barrel of the MP5 over her gimpy left forearm and spun to aim the weapon at me. I bolted like a flushed-out jackrabbit, and bullets kicked up behind me in a stream. I can only guess that her trying to control the small machine gun with one and a half arms was what saved me. Controlling the jumping, chattering firearm was a two-handed job.

I put all the conditioning that I'd been working for into action, sprinting for all I was worth toward the other end of the property. Zigging and zagging every few seconds, I was struck with an idiot urge to scream out "Serpentine! Serpentine!" I refrained. I needed every bit of wind I had to get out in front of team crazy.

I was close to my goal when another stitch pattern of dust-raising rounds raced just past me. I felt a bee-sting on my left side, and prayed it wasn't lethal. I stumbled but kept running until I reached a small section of basalt rock fence that the Spanish sheepherders of long ago had created. I dropped behind it and aimed several rounds back at Marjory the Assassin, making her duck for a moment.

Tactically, this was not the best decision I'd ever made.

She sprayed my position, and it was only distance and her gimpiness that saved me from taking a face full of 9mm parabellum rounds. Nonetheless, I had to dive behind the skimpy rock wall, and dislodged stones fell on my shoulders and back. I couldn't stay there, she'd shoot the un-mortared wall out from in front of me.

It's all but impossible to count rounds when they're coming at you that fast, but I waited for just the right moment. She was spraying me, not bothering to fire in short bursts and many of her rounds went high as the automatic weapon's barrel tried to climb. After a few seconds, I heard the distinct click of an empty chamber.

Once again, the rabbit bolted, firing back at her as I ran.

I was sprinting so fast that I was sure I was leaving a 'rooster tail' of dust behind me. As I neared my destination, I made sure to leave a big slewing track aiming where I was turning, big enough that even a novice tracker couldn't miss the turn.

Just before I reached the doorway, still running, I fired a few wild shots in Marjory's general direction. When I reached the doorway, I sprung upward at the frame, and long-jumped across the space inside the door. My foot touched down lightly once, then I landed on the far side of the 'sweet spot' in the thick sand and fell to my knees.

Glancing back, I was pleased to see that my single track looked like I'd just covered the distance at a sprint and had stumbled, coming to my knees where I was now located. To enhance the bait, I tossed the now-empty Glock by the faint footprint. Hopefully she'd want to grab the firearm I'd been using to shoot a her.

I stood, and trying to leave a frantic-looking track trail, moved around behind the concrete "T" that stood at the end of the concrete kitchen wall. Deciding this wasn't enough protection, I went into the kitchen proper, and looked through a crack where the cast iron stove had once been. I pulled out the decorative little 9mm and waited.

Glancing at the doorless rear entrance for a moment I wondered if she'd try to flank me and come in from that direction. It was unlikely, unless she was the queen of the ninjas, that she'd be able to walk across the broken concrete and basalt, across years of dead dry leaves without me hearing her. But looking back toward the front, through the crack in the wall, left me with an itchy feeling between my shoulder blades.

I needn't have worried. A minute later she called me out.

"Hey, MacKenzie. I hope you're done running, Honey Bun. I looked over the landscape, and there's no fucking place else to go."

I wanted to shout at her. To call *her* out on being the kind of person that would kill someone for money. Fortunately, I'm not quite that stupid. She didn't know for sure where I was, no point in giving her a definite location to start throwing lead.

But, I forgot the lesson of the trailer.

"No answer?" she yelled. "How rude! I hate rudeness in all its forms, MacKenzie. I feel the need to stamp it out whereever I see it." Something plopped into the sand of the front room, and through the crack I saw what she'd thrown in. I dived backward and tried to hug the floor.

An explosion like that is loud. Contained in an enclosed space it is horrifically loud, and all I could hear was the ringing in my own ears. Nothing was visible in the front room, nothing but dust, and through my fingertips I could feel the house groaning and shifting.

Oh God, don't let the roof come down!

Through the ringing I heard a noise at the front door, and the MP5 began spraying the interior. I watched the unprotected walls that weren't behind my concrete barrier jump and pock. Concrete chips flew everywhere. By the time she'd finished the mag, the interior of the old house looked like someone had been target practicing inside for decades.

"You still with me, Mackenzie?" I heard her voice, muffled by my recovering eardrums call out to me. I decided to try to sucker her, and let out a low moan that crescendoed to a sob.

Come and get the poor, wounded, prey, you hell bitch.

I moved to the crack in the wall and aimed the compact semi-auto where the door should be. The dust was starting to settle and I saw her outline in the doorway for a moment, but she knew better than to stay in that space and dashed forward.

There was a huge crashing sound, a thud, a scream of agony.

51

I wasn't about to rush out and see if Operation Tiger Trap had been successful. Just as I'd faked being wounded, the moans I heard from the front room could've been just as false.

I let the dust settle, then slowly and carefully, pistol in a firing grip, moved up to the now gaping hole in the front room's floor. I slowly peeked over the edge, ready to snap my head backward instantly if I needed to.

I didn't need to.

She was lying amongst the rubble on her left side, the MP5 had landed underneath her. A piece of rebar stuck up though her abdomen and another had emerged through her left leg. She was sprawled across broken concrete and for a moment I thought she was dead. She wasn't.

"Oh! God.. Damn... it," She gritted out. "You got me... MacKenzie. Well fucking played, kid. Well... played. I guess you won." Her hand was inching toward the pistol still in its sheath on her right side.

"You touch that gun and I will empty this mag into you."

She pulled her hand back. "Fine kiddo, it's cool. Be cool. You won."

"You're good enough," I replied, "that I'm not about to take any chances with you."

"Why.. Thank you,..Mac. You mind if I call... you Mac? I'm.. a little short of breath... here."

"Everyone else does. Can I ask why the hell you were so determined to kill me?"

"Henh." She coughed, and I noted blood splatter across the stone in front of her. "Real simple. You made a powerful enemy some time back. He hired me, and I... always get my target."

"Not this time," I said, my mind running through the plethora of people who might want me dead.

"Don't be so... sure." I hadn't seen her hand move in the gloom, but now I saw she held something. When I heard the 'pling' sound, I knew what it was. She threw it upward at me.

Years ago, by a fluke of reflex, I had deflected an arrow aimed at my chest with the knife I held. Almost the same thing happened here. I slapped the grenade in mid-air, and it dropped back into the hole with its owner. I threw myself back toward the concrete T and barely cleared it when the ancient house was rocked again by a big blast.

Being below the floor, the sound hadn't been as deafening, but there was still dust everywhere, thicker than London fog. I lay on my back, occasionally coughing, listening to the groaning and creaking of the roof, praying it wouldn't come down. Once again, my prayers were answered.

I got up, and again moved cautiously toward the now larger hole in the floor. Cautiously not because I was worried about the assassin any more, but because I doubted the structural integrity of the remaining flooring.

I'd slammed my shin against the concrete wall in my headlong dive for cover, and it hurt like a beast. No more running for me for a while. Looking into the hole at Marjory, I realized just how lightly I'd gotten off. It took all the willpower I had not to contaminate the crime scene with the contents of my stomach. Thoughts of living by the sword and dying by the sword went through my mind.

She was not a pretty sight. And that is the understatement of the century.

52

He watched the kid come out of the house alone, dust still settling from what had sounded like another grenade going off. Timothy had been hiding in the large rocks at the base of the cliff since before sunrise, knowing if young Mac Crow came to his trailer, it was sure to draw his wayward apprentice. And what he'd seen her do had banished all thoughts of his having trained a professional.

He should've never given her another chance. He should've poisoned Marjory when they'd last met.

He centered the crosshairs of the scope on the young man. He could kill him now with a head shot. Young Crow would never even know he was dead.

He watched him start to stagger up the road, probably still disoriented from the grenade blast, though he didn't look too badly injured. So easy to fulfill Marjory's contract for her.

But no. No, dammit. The young fighter had earned his life. And he'd made it so that Timothy hadn't needed to put a round through Marjory's skull, a task that professional he might be, he hadn't relished doing.

He was getting sentimental in his old age. Definitely time to retire or be retired.

In fact, he decided, he'd start initiating his exit strategy when he returned to his home in Italy. Half his cash accounts were already hidden. Now maybe it was time to set Operation Bora Bora into motion.

In fact, it might be in his best interest to not return home at all.

But before any of that, he was going to have words with one MacKenzie Crow.

53

I walked back to the remains of my trailer, feeling both elated be alive, and horrified that, putting together her various rants, she'd very likely been part of an entire organized association of assassins.

Was she the only one coming? Things that she'd said had indicated that I was a personal hit, but who knew the minds of these kinds of people. Maybe they would come after me purely out of professional "ethics," or maybe one of them would show up on my doorstep simply for revenge for the woman who lay dead behind me.

I needed to get back to Rosa and get her to a hospital. Marjory hadn't bothered with our Subaru, and it was far enough from the trailer to have been unaffected by its explosion.

Though I was weary enough to feel I was carrying the Earth like Atlas was reputed to do, I broke into a trot. The marathon-trained muscles responding after only a few steps, my shin throbbing with every other impact.

As I drew near the trailer, I saw just how much my life had changed. The still smoking airstream was now a 'canoe,' the roof completely gone. The deck was burning and the only thing keeping the fire from spreading was the gravel it was sitting on. Airstreams were built to be cute, not to be bullet and bomb proof. I'd either be bunking with Rosa or my mom for the foreseeable future.

Eighty percent of what I owned was now burning trash. My laptop, my favorite gear, my nature notes and journals, my clothes, all fuel for the fire.

I walked past the burned-out wreck, pushing it out of my mind. All that mattered was getting Rosa out of here and to the hospital. I rounded the stone shed down to the brush patch where I'd left her.

She was gone.

"Rosa! Where are you?" I shouted, panic in my voice.

"She's down here," A male voice said. "By the creek. If you want her to live, I strongly suggest you lose both of your Glocks and any other ordinance that you might've picked up along the way."

I saw Rosa sitting in one of the deck chairs from the shed. Her hands weren't tied but she didn't have her Glock either.

"I have a fairly high-powered weapon aimed at your heart, young man," the voice continued. "Drop those weapons, *now*."

I bent down and set the compact pistol on the lava rock.

"That's all I have. My Glock is at the bottom of a hole with what remains of the woman who came after us. I didn't kill her. She threw a grenade at me, and I swatted it back to her."

"A very fine distinction, indeed. All right, come forward," he said.

Standing up and looking at Rosa, I saw her gesture with her chin to her left and I saw him. His camouflage fatigues and face paint made him very hard to see as he kneeled in the brush along the small creek. I guess that was the point. He gestured with the rifle he was carrying. "Take a seat, MacKenzie. We need to talk."

"You with her? Marjory?" I asked, gesturing toward the end of the road. "Obviously, she... didn't make it."

"Christ, she even told you her name?" I saw he was an older man with a fancy small mustache and a tiny arrow-shaped soul patch under his lip. He shook his head in disgust. "I am part of the same organization. However, I am not here for you. I was here to eliminate her. A failed protege." He sighed. "Young man, I want you to sit next to your lovely friend here. I'm going to tell you how things are going to be."

"Are you going to finish what she started?" Rosa asked. "That's a single shot sniper rifle. You shoot him, and I promise you, you won't get a second shot off."

He smiled as one might at the antics of a toddler. "I assure you, this is not my only weapon, and I have trained long and hard at deploying the others quickly. You, my dear, would have to get to your feet and cover fifteen feet of distance with a piece of shrapnel in your thigh. It would be your last charge."

"There's two of us, and if you're going to kill us anyway, what've we got to lose?" I asked.

"First of all," he said with another sigh, "I have no intention or particular need to shed more blood. I just want to have a little chat, one that I think you'll be glad we had, later down the road."

"Then you have our rapt attention," Rosa told him. "Also, if we're just talking maybe you could lower that rifle."

The man actually laughed. "I don't think so. You two must've rolled tens when it came to luck. I've done a bit of research into your past exploits, and there are a number of people who you should've had no chance against that are now in cemeteries. First rule: take no chances."

"Not to be rude, then," I said. "But she's bleeding, so let's cut to the chase. What do you want from us?"

"I wanted to tell you, that the Association I work for is quite unlikely to come after you again. You see, my former protege cooked this up as a way to try to re-ingratiate herself with our organization after she'd fouled up in a very spectacular way."

"She kept talking about her employer, someone who hated me very much. I assume you guys don't come cheap."

Again the smile, and the man said: "You are quite correct, MacKenzie. Guppies like you two are practically beneath our notice professionally. Marjory felt her only chance to get back in our good graces was to take a years-past underpaid contract from an old enemy of yours. A wealthy one."

"Charles Dallum." I said, unable to keep the bitterness from my voice. I'd made the connection while staring down at Marjory's corpse.

"Very good. Mr. Dallum wanted you dead and tried to enlist Marjory just before he died. She grasped at his contract as a last resort. It was never intended to be anything personal, but it seems my former protege developed a number of bad habits over the years. Flaws that have put my own reputation in serious jeopardy, as I was the one who trained her. The Association is very unforgiving of failure."

"It's good to know these things," Rosa said. "But why? You owe us nothing, and we are loose ends. Not that I want you to tie those loose ends up."

"I deplore waste, and having learned so much about you, I think you two should stay in the gene pool. In a world with so many incredibly gullible and outright stupid people, I think killing two intelligent, creative young people would do no good service to the future of mankind. Silly sentimentalism, but true." He looked at us for a long moment, his camouflaged features making it difficult to really see his expression.

He continued: "Also I do not think either of you know enough to be a threat. Which brings me to the reason for this conversation. I am going to now give you advice for a long and hopefully healthy life."

"Definitely listening," I said.

"I know you want to be outraged. Realizing none of this was your fault, you'll want to seek justice, telling the authorities, local and federal, all about the horrible assassins that you actually know very little about. Here's a single word of advice to live a long life: Don't."

"Because then we won't be beneath their notice."

"Exactly, Ms. Fernandez. As smart as you are, I would suggest that you play as dumb as possible when you get the authorities out here. Say she was some crazy woman who claimed to be a former lover of Mr. Dallum and she wanted revenge. Just make no mention of professional assassins or organizations, and you should be safe."

"And if we should choose not to follow this advice?" I said. Rosa elbowed me in the ribs.

"Really? I know you're not that stupid, but let me spell it out in no uncertain terms, a scenario if you will. You're walking down the streets of the local backwater you call a city. You feel a prick, like a bee sting. Next thing you know, your heart is seizing up and you can't breathe. *Boom*. You're dead of an apparent heart attack before an ambulance can arrive, and all the CPR in the world won't help. No Marjory-style antics, no warning, no trace. You'll be dead. And with what little you know, it would be an absolutely meaningless death."

I nodded. "It's not the first time I've been told to shut up or die. The last time, it was government assassins cleaning up a loose end. I kept my mouth shut then. We'll keep ours shut now." I looked over at Rosa, she nodded. "Neither of us have any desire to swim with the sharks."

"Excellent. I always prefer dealing with intelligent people. As I said, so few of them in the world these days. I think that concludes our business. I'm going to climb out of here and leave. I'll remove her cell-jammer as I go, though with the smoke from your trailer, there may already be fire trucks on the way. You two stay where you are for the next ten minutes. If you try to follow me, it won't go well, which would be a shame after this little talk."

He turned toward the river and walked around the smoking remains of my Airstream, disappearing into the smoke. A few moments later, I heard four "thop" sounds and then complete silence. Even the birds were quiet, as if not wanting to bring attention to themselves.

"What the hell has he done?" I said, starting to rise.

Rosa's grip on my arm stopped me. "Mac. Just. Sit." I saw how pale she was, and sweat beaded her forehead. I glanced down at the piece of aluminum still sticking in her leg.

"How bad?" I asked.

"Not... as bad as Sandra went through during the race. Hardly bleeding, but still hurts like fuck."

"Do we need to..." I gulped. "pull that out?"

"No. Let's let the pros do that. He said he'd kill the jammer, so keep an eye on your burner. As soon as we have service, call me an ambulance, 'kay?"

"Okay."

"In the meantime, we do what the man said. We sit."

54

The call for an ambulance was superfluous.

As I'd been calling for help on my now-working phone, I could already hear sirens in the distance. Fire, medical and sheriff were all on the way already.

As I led the ambulance crew back to where Rosa was still sitting, I noticed that all four tires on the Subaru were flat. Our "advisor" must've had a silenced pistol with him to assassinate our ride out.

They loaded Rosa into the ambulance, asking her all the pertinent questions. As they did that, a kind, very young looking EMT bandaged the nick on my side and my gashed shin. As they drove away toward the hospital with Rosa, I stayed behind and called Uncle Gil.

It went about as I expected.

"You're *where!?*" he shouted. "Dear mother of God, Mac? Why the hell did you come back? Yours is the one place she knew where to find you easily! You should've at least called me. We could've ambushed her with the whole team."

"That was the point, Uncle Gil," I said. "I'm sure she had you all under surveillance of some sort. She'd also threatened to start killing everyone if she thought you were mobilizing. The point was to make it look like we were just touching down for a moment and regrouping. If she saw you and Vinnie and Ed leave your places, she'd never have come for us. And some of you might be dead."

"Jesus! There are so many ways that could have gone wrong. What possessed you to try this? I'd have at least thought Rosa would've had better sense."

"Our stalker made a run at us through an intermediary in Florida. Rosa and I were tired of being on the run. That's not what we wanted for the rest of our lives, and that was what it looked like it was going to be. We wanted to ambush the bitch. Kill or be killed, though I don't want the cops to ever hear that."

"Oh Christ! That was the stupidest thing you could've done. This was a professional, and you say she's dead now? You and Rosa must be the luckiest two punks on God's green Earth."

"Someone else said something similar very recently," I said. "Listen Uncle Gil, the Sheriffs are pulling up. I gotta go. Rosa's being taken to Central Washington Hospital, maybe you can go sit with her while I deal with this. Take Mom along, and Melinda. I'll be there the moment they're done here. Oh, and could you have Vinnie come pick me up? Our ride's been sabotaged."

"Mac, swear to God, if you..."

"Talk to you later, Uncle Gil." I closed the call, as deputy Dave Mathews walked up. Tagging along beside him was Cheryl Bronson, his trainee.

"Holy shit, Mac," Dave said, surveying the remains of my home. "This the work of your stalker?"

"Yeah, it is. Note not only the blown up trailer, but the number of bullet holes in everything. She had an SMG with her. MP5, I think."

"There's a crap ton of brass on the ground, sir," Bronson said. "They look to be 9mm parabellum."

"You said there was a fatality in your call-in. I assume it was him?"

"Her. I'll show you the body, Dave. She chased me to the other end of the property, firing most of the way. It was only the rocks along the road that kept me covered enough not to take one in the back, though I did get nicked in the side." I pointed to the bandage showing through my bloodstained shirt.

We walked along the dust-filled road to the derelict house, Bronson noting and taking photos along the way. There was used brass in the dust most of the way.

"How the hell did she miss you, Mac? This is multiple mags worth of rounds she's expended."

"I rolled a ten for luck, I guess," thinking back on what the assassin, Timothy had said. "But to be fair, she was wounded in the shoulder, and I had almost a sixty-yard head start on her. Also, I had my Glock. I was definitely shooting back."

"And Rosa?"

"I stashed her in the brush along the creek. Our firearms should be right there where she was."

"Cheryl, we'll want to secure those. When our backup gets there, make sure those weapons are picked up."

Dave's words reminded me that I wasn't talking to my friend at the moment, but instead, to law enforcement. We reached the house, and I cautioned them about the weak floor before we went in.

"So she followed you in and fell through the floor here? Did you intend for this to work as a trap?"

I wasn't about to admit any sort of premeditation, even though this was so obviously self-defense. Word to the wise, always be careful what you admit to and how you word things when talking to law enforcement.

"Dave, I was trying to draw the crazy bitch away from Rosa. That was my only plan. I was surely trying to shoot her, defending myself, but look around. This house was literally the only place to hide." I was feeling very happy that I'd never gotten around to making the warning sign about the danger here.

"Yeah, you definitely got yourself cornered here. And if you'd run up the hill I'm pretty sure she'd have got you in the back. At least, that's how it'll be in my report."

As Dave and I stood talking outside the house, I saw that trainee Bronson had decided to take a look. "Officer, you might want to brace yours..."

Bronson looked down into the gaping holes, enlarged by the grenade, and I saw her horrified expression. A moment later, she spun and expended her lunch into the blackberry brush.

"That bad?" Dave said.

"She was wounded bad when I looked down to see what happened to her. The psycho tried to throw a grenade at me, and it hit the edge of the floor. It bounced back to her."

He grimaced and went to take a look. We leaned over the edge of the destroyed floor and looked down at Marjory. The view hadn't improved in the least.

"Eeesh," he said. "What a mess. Looks like several mags and the aforementioned MP5 are down there... and are those what I think they are lying next to her?"

"Yes. Extra grenades as far as I can tell. If they'd gone off in the blast the entire foundation might've gone and dropped the roof on me."

"Shit oh dear," Dave replied. "Cheryl, you with us?"

"I'm good, sir. Sorry sir."

"Don't worry about it. That's a horrific sight. Get on the

radio and tell dispatch we are going to need the bomb squad out here. Tell them multiple unexploded grenades that have been 'stressed' surrounding a corpse. Location is remote so no civilians to worry about, but the detectives aren't gonna want to touch this while there's live ordinance at the incident scene." Dave looked at me sideways. "You sure are making our bomb unit earn their keep, Mac."

"I'd point out that it was her who was playing with big bang stuff." I said. "Not me."

We began the walk back toward the still smoldering trailer. A fire truck had made it down the switchbacked driveway and was filling the canoe-shaped remains of the Airstream with water. Rivers were running out of multiple gaps in the destroyed floor.

"Mac," Dave said. "It seems obvious that this was self-defense, but, as a friend, I strongly suggest you lawyer-up before you give a statement. Chelan county may get its share of petty crimes and the occasional murder, but this is pretty spectacular. Protect yourself."

"Good advice, thanks."

55

Dave's advice had been sound. Detective Messner, a lean ascetic man with bruised looking eye sockets, had grilled both Rosa and me pretty thoroughly. I was very glad to have Marilee Roberts, Chambers and Associate's on-retainer legal counsel, there with us. Messner had seemed to take it as a personal affront that this had happened in his jurisdiction.

He also had a problem with the way that Rosa and I made our living. Bounty hunting was something he didn't think should be allowed by the law, but in the end, all he could do was admit that all the evidence pointed to self-defense. Our earlier contacts with the police about someone stalking me helped, as well as the bomb under Rosa's RAV. And when someone comes to kill you with an automatic weapon and several grenades, it's hard to argue that you're not justified in killing them to stay alive.

Rosa was up and around, limping slightly but the metal that had lodged itself in her leg had hit nothing but muscle. But now, she, who'd made it through war and psychos and bail jumpers without any major wounds, had her first sizable scar.

She and our former running mentor, Sandra, had something in common now.

And me? I was homeless.

Yeah, I know. Being a drama queen about it, but dammit, I loved that trailer.

I actually had my pick of multiple places to stay and was lucky enough that the love of my life made that decision for me.

"Mac, you're staying at my place while you figure out how to get something back out there to live in. Besides," her voice dropped to barely audible, "maybe it'll be practice for later on down the road?" I surely didn't object.

As for the Association, we followed the stranger with the rifle's advice. We did everything we could to enhance the narrative that Marjory had been a psycho stalker, not a member of a professional corps of world-class assassins. I hoped the stranger's advice was sound. Neither Rosa nor I relished the idea of looking over our shoulders for the rest of our lives.

Some might say it was our duty to tell the feds everything. I would say in return that what little we did know wouldn't be anything more than what the government very likely already knew. What we could tell them was actually quite small.

Lastly, neither Rosa nor I, Uncle Gil or Vinnie (who are the only ones we told everything) felt our government's three-letter agencies could protect us. Marjory's vast information access, that allowed her to find and track us, could only mean the Association of assassins had to have operatives bought and paid for in our own government.

I don't want to seem like a coward, but as Clint Eastwood once said, "A man's got to know his limitations."

56

A month later, I was standing on a semi-freshly poured pad of concrete on the spot where my Airstream had sat before it was hauled away to the junkyard. I'd spent a week making trips to the dump, getting rid of scrap and the burnt remains of my possessions.

It hadn't been a total loss. Some of my most prized possessions had been outdoor stuff gifted to me by Ed, Uncle Gil and my mom. Most of that had been stored in the shed simply because I had to carefully pick and choose what lived with me in the twenty-foot airstream.

I'd had a few tubs of clothes in the shed, but most of those were old, and I'd literally outgrown them. Rosa had taken me shopping, seemingly a regular activity in our relationship. There were some disagreements there. Let's just say we had differing opinions on style and leave it at that.

Now, sitting there on a crisp November day, we were waiting.

"I think I hear it," Rosa said from the new Adirondack-style chairs we'd been sitting in.

"Yep. We better clear the deck," I said, picking up the

small outdoor table with our drinks sitting on it. We moved it and the chairs thirty yards toward the river, not wanting anything sitting on or near the concrete pad.

The *thap thap thap* sound coming up the river soon directed our sight to a small spot in the sky that was enlarging quickly. Then it turned into two spots in the sky, one below the other. These resolved into a very, very large helicopter and a flying motorhome.

"That chopper alone took all the insurance money," I said, shading my eyes in the bright sunlight.

"At least the motorhome was free," Rosa replied, "assuming that such a vehicle can ever be considered truly *free*. Vinnie said that they're a hole in the road that you throw money into."

"Uncle Gil said the motor on that thing is a total write off. When he and Ed offered it to me as my new home, no strings attached I said 'heck yeah,' wouldn't you?"

"Maybe, but I'm going to miss sharing the apartment with you. On the other hand, with the king-sized bed in that thing I am much more likely to come out here for extended stays."

"Double extra bonus points for the motorhome, then." As I said it, Vinnie's Bronco and Uncle Gil's SUV came down the switchbacked driveway to my place. "I won't mind having Uncle Gil's help getting the thing set in place."

It took another fifteen minutes with the pilot and him conversing by radio to get the motorhome settled in just right, perfectly aligned with the concrete slab. Then carrying cables and straps were unhooked, hauled up, and the pilot went back down the river in a curving arc for home.

I'd paid a contractor to rebuild the water, power and septic connections and we spent the rest of the afternoon getting everything hooked up and running. Part of that was deflating the tires and blocking the big vehicle for stability.

Hydraulic stabilizers were put in place, and slide-outs were extended. The "motor" home was ready for habitation.

With me, Rosa, Uncle Gil, Ed and Melinda, Vinnie and my mom in the new place, it still didn't seem that crowded. The thing was that big.

"You know," Mom said, taking the steaks out of a cooler that we'd later be grilling down by the riverfront. "A home this nice, Mac, you might want to give it a name."

"Name it *Enterprise*," Vinnie said. "It's certainly big enough."

"It's a stationary object now, Vincent," Rosa said. "And I'm pretty sure that my man will want to name it something beautiful. Give him time to think about it."

"I already know what I want to name it," I said. "A perfect name."

Everyone looked at me, waiting to hear it.

"It's what I've always called this place. Let's call it Paradise."

———

The End.

AFTERWORD

One of the benefits of having lived an interesting life is that as an author, you can draw on all those interesting events and "enhance" them for your novels.

Case in point: the scene in this novel with the Black Pickup of Death. While in college at Washington State University, I needed extra money to survive, and worked for Dominos Pizza to supplement my income. WSU was just across the border from Moscow, Idaho, and the the road between the two was a place to be cautious. Idaho had a lower drinking age than Washington State and underclassmen had a habit of going over there to over-indulge themselves at the local bars. They also tended to drive home under the influence.

I was driving to the Moscow Dominos to deliver some supplies in my somewhat dilapidated Mustang one dark night, when, just as in Mac's story, a black pickup came at me head-on. No lights and on my side of the road. Fortunately, my reflexes were good and I managed to hug the shoulder far enough out that the truck missed my car by inches. I was also luckier in that I didn't lose control and kept the car on the road, albeit with a lot of fishtailing by the Mustang's rear end.

The part about watery knees was also accurate. When I reached my destination, I had to lean on my car to stay on my feet when I got out.

In the novel you just read, Mac tells Rosa about a story his Sensei Dade told him. Mac promised to tell the story later.

Now, it's later. And yes, it's based on something that happened to me.

———

-Clint

———

———

(Note: I was the one who proofread this particular text. Any errors are mine, and mine alone.)

———

Sensei Dade's Story

———

I was showered and dressing in the small locker room, Sensei Dade just a few lockers away, when it occurred to me to ask something.

"Sempai, remember when you first started helping me with these personal training sessions?" I asked. "After slamming me to the floor all those times in sparring? That was a 'nail sticking up' moment, wasn't it?"

"Henh, The Nail That Sticks Up Gets Hammered Down," Dade said, "No Mac, not so much. Sensei Uchida just felt you needed a course correction, and asked me to see to it. When you wrap that black piece of cloth around your middle, all your lessons get harder."

"I still remember seeing stars while my course was being corrected. So, if I may ask, did you ever have a 'course correction' of your own?"

Dade hesitated. I wasn't the first of the students junior to him to try to get a karate story out of him, and I could see him him weighing the benefits and detriments to answering my question. He must've seen something in the idea that might be useful for me to learn.

"Well, Mac. I started my karate 'career' at Washington State, where I met Sensei Uchida. I found I took to our art like a duck takes to water, maybe even becoming a little bit fanatical with training." From his expression, I could see his mind wandering corridors of the past, and his dark face broke out in a grin. "So, I thought if training in one martial art was good, training in two would be better. So I started Kendo."

"The sword art?"

"The modern sport form of Japanese sword. Japan's version of modern fencing."

"How did it go? I thought Sensei said we shouldn't train in another art until after black belt."

"Well," he said, expression wry, "it could have gone better."

He looked at a locker, not really seeing it. "I joined the university kendo club and the sensei there was a woman who was also an exchange student in the grad program. She was from Japan, and apparently fairly highly ranked in Kendo. An American teacher might have handled things differently, but since this was a Japanese art, I guess she decided that we should all just know how things should be through osmosis, I guess. I came in, all full of enthusiasm, bringing my own red oak training sword, which I learned was not much good for actual contact. It was broken by blocking a senior's practice stroke later on."

I noted that few of the training weapons we had in our dojo were made of red oak.

"For the first few months," he continued, "All we did was learn to shift-glide up and down the floor. I actually built fairly thick calluses on my feed, just from that. But if I'm honest, the monotony of it began to wear after the first month. In our Karate system, at the end of the first month, students at least have a few stances, the first three blocks and the first three strikes. At the end of the first two months under her tutelage, I knew how to shift my weight."

"Wow. How did she keep students?"

"Understand, Mac, that this is the traditional way of doing things in Japan. I didn't understand that at the time. I might have handled things differently in hindsight. Age and perspective can alter how you think about things. Though... I can't say for certain that I was wrong about some of the things I thought, either."

"Were there many students?"

"The class wasn't very big, so being shunted off to the side to work on stances by myself for over a month didn't make much sense. I figured it was some test of patience, and if I just lasted, if I was patient, things would get better."

"And did it?" I asked.

"After a month and a half, I started to wonder if it was me, or maybe the color of my skin. I began to think I was being ignored simply to get me to leave."

I didn't know how to answer that. My ancestry was pretty much lily white, and I lived in an area where African Americans comprised about 1% of the total population.

"So, what happened?"

"After two months, I very politely asked if I could begin working with the sword, maybe do a little kumité with the other low-ranking students. I was told that the sensei would decide that, and to just get back over to my little corner. The only thing that kept me from being sure it was about race was that my friend Dave had gone with me. He was the same rank as I was, but was as caucasian as the day was long. He wasn't treated much better, and now, in retrospect, it may have been because we has shown up in our Karate uniforms. Those were all we had, and fifteen years later, I still don't know if that had any bearing on the situation."

I started to reply, then decided this was not the time to interrupt the flow of what was beginning to be a good story.

"At three months, we were taught the most rudimentary upper block, and the basic overhead strike. We began to do this like the repetitions that we'd done before, sliding up and down the dojo only now, we got to take our hands off our hips and swing our arms around."

"For another month?" I asked.

"Oh no. Three more months, still doing the same thing, almost the entire class. All the students ahead of us, even those only a few months our senior, now had Bogu and..."

"Bogu?"

"The armor used in the sport. A cloth helmet with a face guard, a bamboo rib guard and these little mitts to protect the hands. Anyway, even the people a little ways ahead, that had started only a month before had not only been working on a variety of techniques, but now were being integrated into basic sparring, with careful guidance from the seniors. Dave and I were getting the message. We just weren't really wanted there. I'm pleased to say that it was Dave who first suggested we pack it in and hit the bricks. It showed uncommon good sense on his part."

"And did you?"

"Dave did," Dade said. "And in my heart, I knew he was right, but I went ahead and asked the senior student, where the sensei could hear me, if I too could do a little sparring. I noted the look that the senior sent to the sensei, and if I'd have had any sense, I'd have been at least mentally prepared for what came next."

"That doesn't sound good." I noted.

Dade smiled slightly, "I was told it would be allowed, and I was loaned a set of Bogu and a Shinai, the split bamboo training sword they use. My first inkling that I was in trouble, was when the most senior student stepped out into the match area instead of one of my fellow beginners. Keep in mind, that even the other white belt beginners had been getting some sparring in, and any one of them could probably have beaten a student who'd only learned one strike, one block and basic floor movement. The senior stepped out, face hidden by his helmet, and the others helped me into the kendo armor. We both stepped out into the ring, and I was hoping beyond hope that he was going to give me some instruction. All I received, was the basic rules from the referee and then it was go-time."

"Oh man..." I said.

"We squared off, and I held the split bamboo shinai sword in front of me, like I saw my opponent doing and tried to prepare. The ref said "*Hajimē*" to start the match, and my position was explained to me. I didn't even see his sword move before it was curving at high impact over the top of my head. Oh... the stars... He hit me so hard, my knees actually buckled a little. This was hammering the nail in actuality."

"Was that the end of it?"

"Oh no. It was a three point match. They all watched impassively as regained my wits and pride wasn't going to allow me to show any more weakness. I knew how it was going to go, but I figured I could survive at least the next two points. We squared off again, the ref started us and WHAM! He did the exact same thing and though I saw it coming this time, I couldn't get my sword up to block fast enough. More stars, and I almost went down to one knee, with the pain in my head. They watched me stagger with no expression, none at all."

"I might have bowed out at that point." I said.

"That would have been the smart move, but when has pride ever been smart? What happened was that I started to burn inside. I knew there wasn't a bit of this that was fair and I also knew there was nothing I could do about it except quit. Instead of that, I got mad."

"What'd you do?"

"I determined, just like the samurai of old, that if I couldn't win, I wouldn't lose. If I was going down and there was no way around it, my opponent was going down with me. We set, the ref told us to start and I saw it coming in, the same painful strike. Instead of trying to stop it, I stepped into it and thrust the tip of my bamboo sword forward. Right into his throat guard and while his strike hit me, it was not nearly as hard as before. The senior went over backwards, and landed on his back coughing like crazy."

"Whoa!"

"The sensei was in my face seconds later, telling me that was a black belt technique, and not ever to be used by anyone else due to the danger. She was pissed. For one, I had injured her most senior student, and second, her 'lesson' had back-fired. I went over to the edge of the mat to remove my armor, and one of the brown belts came over and told me I was not to come back. I bowed out, left and that was the end of my kendo career."

"That's intense. Were you okay with that?"

Sensei Dade looked at me for a moment, as if weighing his words carefully. "Maybe I should have felt bad, Mac, but if

I'm to be completely truthful with you, I don't. Whatever it was that she wanted me to learn, it wasn't what I actually learned."

"What was the take away then?"

"I could go into things like not letting someone else dictate the field of battle, Mac, but really I think the thing to learn from this is simple. There comes a time when you see you're on a path that's just wasting the finite minutes of your life. Know when to quit and try something else. That and always keep an eye on the one in charge."